An ache moved through him like a thunderstorm across the nighttime jungle...

"Fox, can you feel my emotions right now?"

"Yes, I can. That is the beauty of being twin flames."

"Do you feel as I'm feeling right now?"

"Yes. I have been in this emotional state of longing for you since I died and passed into spirit."

"This...this...need, longing, has never gone away?"

"No, Beloved, it has not."

"I feel like my heart is tearing itself apart with the thought of not having you near me."

"I'm sorry that this has happened. I was wrong to initiate this connection. I see that now. I didn't want you to feel pain. Only my love for you."

Aella sighed with frustration. Unconsciously she rubbed the area over her heart. *This is intense. Yet, it makes me feel more alive than I have ever been...*

Dear Readers,

I love writing on the WARRIORS FOR THE LIGHT series! This time around, I wanted to look into the fascinating question of "soul mates." Do you believe that there is a man for you that is your "other half"? Have you ever met someone that you were helplessly drawn to and could not resist if you tried? Has another man made you feel the center of his universe, that his love for you transcends time and space?

Well, if you have either had this experience or heard of someone else who did, I hope you will find *Reunion* a powerful story of love lost found again—only in different life times. And, even worse, Atok Sopa, the hero who is an Incan Jaguar Warrior, finds his beloved, but now she is in another lifetime. And he has made different choices in the dimension in which he lives.

When you find your soul mate, what do you do? What ends would you go to in order to reconnect with that person? Would laws and rules stand in your way? Come and join me as we watch Atok Sopa wrestle with these very real questions. Even worse, the woman he has never stopped loving is now the focus of the Dark Lord. And Victor Guerra will stop at nothing, not even murdering her, to get the vaunted emerald sphere that she is seeking to find.

Warmly,

Lindsay McKenna

REUNION

LINDSAY McKENNA

All the characters in this book have no existence outside the imagination of
the author, and have no relation whatsoever to anyone bearing the same name
or names. They are not even distantly inspired by any individual known or
unknown to the author, and all the incidents are pure invention.

First published in Great Britain 2011
Harlequin Mills & Boon Limited,
Eton House, 18-24 Paradise Road, Richmond, Surrey TW9 1SR

© Lindsay McKenna 2010

ISBN: 978 0 263 87925 4

89-0111

Harlequin Mills & Boon policy is to use papers that are natural, renewable
and recyclable products and made from wood grown in sustainable forests.
The logging and manufacturing processes conform to the legal environmental
regulations of the country of origin.

Printed and bound in Spain
by Litografía Rosés S.A., Barcelona

As a writer, **Lindsay McKenna** feels that telling a story is a way to share what and how she sees the world that she lives in. Love is the greatest healer of all and the books she creates are parables that underline this belief. Working with flower essences, another gentle healer, she devotes part of her life to the world of Nature to help ease people's suffering. She knows that the right words can heal and that creation of a story can be catalytic to a person's life. And in some way she hopes that her books may educate and lift the reader in a positive manner. She can be reached at www.lindsaymckenna.com or www.medicinegarden.com.

To my sister ROMVETS, women who have proudly served in the military armed forces. And thank you, Merline Lovelace, for your friendship and being a stellar force among us. You're a great role model. I hope readers will check your website out at: www.merlinelovelace.com. I continue to learn from you.

And Rae Monet, former FBI agent, RWA winner and all around good gal, thank you for your help with TIME RAIDERS by developing a beautiful website for our ROMVET series! www.timeraidersseries.com. Rae continues to show her creativity not only in her books, but in creating websites. http://raemonetinc.com. You gals epitomize military "can do" spirit, teamwork and supporting others. I wish I could give you a trophy honouring you, but maybe this dedication can, in some small way, thank both of you for your generosity and team spirit to help so many others.

And thank you to all the ROMVET authors who helped us get TIME RAIDERS up and off the ground. http://www.romvets.com. I'm so fortunate to be among such a creative, intelligent group of women who are true professionals in our field of endeavor.

Chapter 1

"Come here, Chaska...." Atok Sopa breathed, reaching for his wife. They lived in a cozy hut, and he could tell by the light leaking around the cracks of the wooden door that dawn was breaking. It was July, and the weather atop Machu Picchu, the winter residence of Emperor Pachacuti, was warm in comparison to the summer palace in Cusco. This beautiful temple site was at six thousand feet and reminded Atok of a warm blanket.

As he sought his young wife, Atok felt his

loins hardening with need of her once again. They'd been married by Emperor Pachacuti himself, a very special blessing. As a jaguar warrior, Atok's entire life was devoted to protecting his emperor.

He brushed his wife's arm beneath the alpaca blanket with his fingertips. She had pulled the thickly woven fabric across her naked form. Smiling to himself, Atok heard her whisper his name like a prayer. Such was the love they had for one another. Atok had fallen for his black-haired, brown-eyed wife when she was all of eight years old; now she was twenty. Chaska was from royal blood and a part of Pachacuti's Incan court. Atok had been ten years old and preparing for another brutal test of his clairvoyant powers in order to be accepted into the jaguar warrior-training program. That's when he'd spotted her.

As his hand contacted the smooth, warm flesh of her upper arm and then trailed languidly downward, Atok remembered that first day he'd seen her. Chaska's family was part of Pachacuti's larger family circle. She was nobility. He was from a line of warriors and far below her in rank. On that fateful day, he'd watched her run like a graceful alpaca across the green length of Machu Picchu, her thin, long arms spread upward to touch the ragged wisps of fog that lingered above the magnificent stone city. Her stride, her determination had sealed his destiny. Chaska's black hair was straight and fell to her waist. On that day, it flew behind her proud shoulders like a gleaming ebony banner. Her light-brown eyes, slightly tilted, were ablaze with wonder. A child wrapped in awe, Atok had watched her as thirstily as a llama who had not seen water in days. She was irresistible!

Sighing over the sweet memories, Atok allowed his fingers to gently graze Chaska's long back. Even now, she was like the graceful alpaca, a long, lovely neck, aristocratic features—high cheekbones, a straight nose and full lips. Oh, how he'd pined for her secretly in his heart from that first day.

Only after he'd passed his last life-death initiation had the old priest, Chima, informed him that the emperor was giving him Chaska in marriage as a graduation gift. Atok had nearly passed out from the thrill of that unexpected pronouncement from the aged priest.

He recalled how frightened he'd been shortly after that. What if Chaska's family refused the match? A jaguar warrior was elevated to the status of nobility even if they had commoner's blood. After all, Atok had shown his skills and he'd survived the last test that had killed seventy-five percent of the supplicants.

A bit of a smile pulled at his mouth as he heard Chaska's breathing change. Good, she was awakening. Atok was away six months out of the year during the dry season, fighting at the emperor's side. That was when Pachacuti pushed his thousands of soldiers north to Ecuador and south to Chile, to keep a firm hand on the hundreds of different peoples who comprised his far-flung empire. For now, the emperor was in residence. That gave Atok a well-earned few weeks rest with his wife, who loved him as fiercely as he loved her.

"Oh, Fox. You interrupted my dreams...." Chaska turned onto her back and gazed up into her young husband's deeply shadowed face. The faint light of the dawn showed the strength of his square-jawed face, those dark, slightly slanted obsidian eyes that glinted like a jaguar's, the many scars he'd taken in the name of his emperor over the last few years.

Chaska reached up and lightly dragged her nails against his broad, powerful chest. Even in the dim light, she could see the ripple and hardening of his muscles wherever she stroked his firm flesh. Through her thick lashes, she saw his eyes change, narrow, and her breath hitched with anticipation. He'd been gone for three months and she'd missed him so much that she'd thought her heart would break. Now, he was home. He was here, beside her in their newly created stone home.

"My jaguar likes my touch," she teased throatily, rolling over. As she did, the dark-brown alpaca blanket rode off her shoulders to her hips, exposing her upper body. Chaska hungered for the taste of Atok's lips. His kisses inflamed her, filling her body with a raging fire.

With a growl, Atok brought his arm around his wife's waist and drew her to him on their llama wool pallet.

"My lord," Chaska laughed softly, pressing her small breasts into his chest, "I can feel how hungry you are."

Atok drowned in her eyes and couldn't hold back anymore. "I've missed you." He took her mouth roughly. Her lips gave and took in return. Chaska was no compliant little girl. She had retained her childhood's wild spirit as she had grown into a beautiful and desirable young woman. Atok knew she had had many suitors, even a prince or two among them. And yet the emperor had given her to him. How had he known of his love for Chaska? Atok was sure the emperor was just as clairvoyant as any of his jaguar warriors. Atok had never talked about his love for Chaska—ever. And it had been a special hell keeping his mind focused on his many trials and challenges to sharpen his psychic skills. There was no way he could have allowed his mind to wander or he'd have died during the harsh schooling.

Her mouth opened and he tasted honey, felt her smile. He absorbed the rest of her slender form undulating against him like the mighty anaconda that ruled the rivers, lakes and streams of the Incan empire. The pressure of her thighs and rounded belly against his hard-ness made him groan. The vibration rippled up through him and surrounded them as she eagerly filled his mouth with her searching, dart-ing tongue. He loved her wildness, her sense of freedom.

But then, his spirit guide was a jaguar. It made sense that the woman given to him would be equally wild in other ways to com-plement his skills. He felt her tongue boldly move against his flat lower lip. Her fingers trailed like droplets of soft, warm rain across his thickly muscled shoulders. Chaska's hand ranged across his hard ribcage to his flat belly. When her fingers dove through the dark hair surrounding his hardness, he clenched his teeth and sucked air between them. Eyes shuttering closed, Atok felt the ministrations of her hand sliding provocatively around his thickness and teasingly exploring him. She laughed into his mouth and broke their kiss.

"Now, mighty jaguar, you can see who rules you." She smiled into his glittering eyes. Indeed, Atok was powerful as few men would ever be. He was virile, commanding and yet a thoughtful lover toward her. Chaska leaned up and brushed her breasts against his chest. Her nipples were hard. How she longed for him to suckle them.

As if reading her mind, he twisted onto his back. His arms were strong, and he lifted her as if she were lighter than wind so that her long legs could straddle him. "If that's true, come, sit on me. Ride me."

The invitation was heated and Chaska

laughed breathily as she splayed her fine fingers across his barrel-like chest. She sighed
and slowly engulfed his length. Her body,
though small, accommodated his masculine
power. As he filled her, her eyes closed and she
braced herself for the mounting pleasure. Atok
sat up and she rocked between his long, hard
thighs. His mouth sought and found one of her
breasts. Her body shuddered with ecstasy as
his lips closed around the bud and he began to
suckle her strongly. That sensation sent a bolt
of pleasure straight into her loins. Instantly, her
body tightened like a fist around him. They
groaned together, enjoying the incredible heat
swirling through their joined bodies.

Atok felt his wife trembling as her fingers
dug into his taut shoulders. He could taste the
sweet liquid coaxed from each of her nipples.
She rode him with cries of joy and surprise
and an immense vortex of energy built in his
loins. They had been married three years. They
yearned mightily for a child to complete them
as a family.

Holding Chaska as she shuddered through one orgasm after another, breathing raggedly, their heads pressed against one another, their arms in mutual embrace, Atok knew his beautiful wife was now pregnant. As she experienced her last orgasm and then fainted against him, Atok gently eased her limp form off and laid her beside him. He quickly drew several alpaca blankets over them and lay down beside her. Sliding his arm beneath Chaska's neck, Atok rolled her toward him so that the furnace-like heat radiating from his body would keep her warm. Sweat trickled between them, melted together and was absorbed by the blankets.

Soon, Chaska revived. She weakly placed her arm around his neck and nuzzled deep beneath his jaw. Atok had never felt such fulfillment as he did in this moment. He burned that memory into his spirit and his soul. This was an event he never wanted to forget. To create a little spirit out of pure love was the ultimate goal to Atok. A child created in love would go on to live a loving life. Chaska had been so created, for her parents were blindly and happily in love with one another to this day. That is what Atok desired. Many never attained such a state. Now, with his lovely wife pressed along the length of him, her body flush against his harder angles, Atok experienced giddiness. His dream of having a child would come true.

Inhaling his musky scent, Chaska whispered, "You always take me to the wings of the condors. I feel as if I am riding up and down the mighty, invisible currents that they float upon far above us."

Chuckling indulgently, Atok breathed in his wife's special perfume. An old woman priestess, Elona, gathered special orchids at certain times of the year and made scents that seemed other-worldly. The one that Chaska loved was spicy. It infused him with a desire to mate with Chaska over and over again. Perhaps she'd worn that fragrance last night in hopes that he would be so inspired. "A jaguar warrior and a condor woman. What do they have in common, I ask you."

She giggled softly and kissed his neck, his jaw and then leaned up to capture his smiling mouth. Sliding her lips against his, she gloried in his strength and his indescribable gentleness. Atok was nearly six feet tall, heavily muscled and one of the emperor's mightiest warriors, yet he held her like a little rescued bird. "Well, you may be a famous jaguar warrior, but your name, Atok, means fox. You are really a fox in the guise of a jaguar, my dear husband. You rule the earth and all four-legged creatures. I rule the air." She raised her brows and gave him a humorous look. "That is why we can get along."

Moving his hand between them, his long, strong fingers following the curve of her belly, he said thickly, "On this dawn we have created a child, beloved. Our child. Finally…"

Chaska gazed into his warm dark eyes. "Yes…I know. I felt it, too."

* * *

Atok jolted out of his sleep. The dream hung around him like a call of a siren. His heart pounded with anguish. He'd never stopped aching from the loss of Chaska. Sitting up, he looked around. Now in the fourth dimension and a guardian-in-training to the Great Serpent Mound in North America, he sighed heavily. Atok rubbed his face and tried to awaken. Chima, the guardian, was away on training. He would return shortly. By earth time, it would be three weeks, Atok guessed.

He wanted to go back and relive the dream of loving Chaska once again. Oh, how he missed her! It pained him to wake up and find the emptiness. He looked around the quiet site where the great snake had been built by men. It was dawn, and he appreciated this time on Earth. Now, as a spirit guardian, he no longer had to continue reincarnating down to the third-dimensional world that he saw around him. Still, he missed it. Because of Chaska. Because he had lost her during childbirth. Atok had been there and had watched the baby come out of her too-small body, the cord wrapped around his neck. He was dead upon delivery. And then Chaska had bled to death despite all that the learned priestesses could do.

That day was forever branded on his soul. Atok would never forget it. He had held his tiny blue-faced son in his mighty arms and cried. He had held the little child naked against his body, his tears falling upon the quiet face and nostrils that would never breathe. Eventually, a priestess came and gently placed a white alpaca blanket around his son and eased him out of Atok's shaking arms.

For the rest of that nightmare day, he had held Chaska, rocked her, wept and cried out her name. Atok lost count of hours or days. When the priestess was able to get him to release the love of his life, she had grown stiff and unmoving. Even the emperor Pachacuti had come to his hut, talked quietly with him and urged Atok to come with him. The emperor had put his arm around his shoulders and led him toward the cave where all jaguar warriors took their final initiation. It was a cave of life and death, just as the mighty jaguar of the Incan empire ruled over life and death.

Atok had little memory of what the emperor had said to him, of the brotherly way he had treated him or of the compassion given to him after Chaska's body was burned at the Moon Temple and her spirit sent on to the other realm. He had no more tears left to give her as he stood in the upper square where the temples were located. The white-robed priestesses who manned the Moon Temple sang beautifully. The goblet of ayahuaska vine, a hallucinogen, was passed to Atok. He shook his head. He was a jaguar warrior. He had the psychic skills to see Chaska in spirit. The knowledge that she would choose to move into the fourth dimension to rest three days after she left the physical body, made his heart ache with incredible mountains of loneliness. Atok simply didn't know how he could continue to survive in this world without her. The baby that they'd created on that special

morning made him weep after the ceremony.
He would never get to welcome that little spirit
into the earth realm. Atok's life went from
rainbows to a grayness that remained with
him until he was killed in battle the following
spring. He'd leapt upward to take a spear that
had been thrown at his emperor during a particularly savage battle north of Cusco.

As the spear had slammed into Atok's chest,
he had felt the iron point pierce his heart. An
explosion of warmth and blood had spurted out
of his chest. Atok fell to the ground, knowing
full well he was dying. And, as a jaguar warrior, he was able to feel the silver cord dissolv-
ing and releasing his spirit from that physical
vehicle they called Atok Sopa.

At the moment of death, when he rose out
of the third dimension and into the fourth dimension, how badly he wanted to meet with
Chaska! But that was not to be. Instead, he was
met by Grandmother Alaria and Grandfather
Adaire. They were the leaders of the Village
of the Clouds, a place where he had been taken

from time to time in his training to become a jaguar warrior. This was the stronghold of the *Taqe*, People of the Light who battled the *Tupay* or People of heavy energy.

With sunlight blazing around her white-robed form, her silver hair sparkling, Alaria smiled and held her hand out to Atok. "My son, welcome home. Your earthly existence is at an end for this lifetime. We welcome you across the bridge and to our other world."

Grasping her long, lean fingers, Atok walked over the wooden bridge that arched above the small stream. Adaire smiled at him and placed his hand on Atok's shoulder as he stood with them. Around him was a jungle but also a path, a familiar one to him, leading to the village itself. It wasn't a long walk. They brought him between them.

"I want to see Chaska," he said, looking around. "I thought I'd see her once I'd died."

"My son, she has already reincarnated. She's in another body on Earth. I'm sorry...."

Adaire told him, giving him a look of sad understanding.

Atok continued to walk between his favorite mentors. They had once been Druids and had been the leaders on the Isle of Mona before it had been attacked and destroyed by the Romans so long ago. That was their last lifetime of incarnation. From there, because of their saintly attributes, they were given the heavy responsibility of the Village of the Clouds. Atok knew this center of light energy was the vital heart of the fourth-dimensional world where all *Taqe* spirits went after dying and leaving the earthly plane. It was here that spirits came for further training, tutoring, education and healing. Even people still living on the earth plane could visit here—and did—in astral travel, in their dreams, to receive further training on spiritual subjects.

"Where has Chaska reincarnated?" he asked.

Alaria shook her head, her hand going around his left arm and squeezing it gently. "You cannot know that, Atok. She is fine."

"Is she happy?" For he was not.

Adaire sighed. "Happiness is not a hallmark of earth-plane existence, my son. You know that. Earth is a schoolroom, a very hard class where a soul wants to rub off the hard edges and gain quick education."

"True," Alaria said in a low tone. "Atok, you know that a soul can choose to go anywhere in our dimension to gain knowledge and spiritually evolve. And you know that the earth classroom is considered the hardest, the most severe albeit the quickest education for a soul who really wants to ascend to the master level."

Atok knew all of that, but he still felt miserable. The path opened up and he saw the familiar peaks of many thatched roofs from the village up ahead. A peace descended upon his weary spirit. In three days he could release this personality and move into pure spirit once more. That was a choice he had. Yet he had loved his life as a jaguar warrior more than any other and did not want to release it just yet.

All those who left a physical body "burned

off" their personality of that lifetime. A soul could create five, ten, twenty different personalities and go into that many lifetimes at once. And the lives didn't have to be on Earth, either. An incarnation could be to a chosen star, a constellation, planets or galactic systems or, indeed, in other dimensions. A soul that hungered to regain oneness with the Creator often sent many energy pieces of themselves into new Earthly incarnations and bodies. Not all souls did that, of course. Atok was aware that his soul was one of those which desired the connection with the Creator sooner rather than later.

"Why can I not reincarnate to where Chaska has gone?" he demanded almost petulantly.

"Because you have other choices to consider," Adaire said. They halted at a hut. "This is where you will live for now, Atok."

"What are my choices?" he pressed.

Alaria smiled slightly. "Atok, you are at a level where you no longer need to have physical incarnations. You have evolved and we are offering you training to become a guardian of a sacred site located on Earth. You can take this new path or go back and continue physical incarnation. But it will never be in the same life as Chaska."

His heart squeezed with such pain that Atok hung his head and pressed his hand against his chest. Never to see Chaska again? Lifting his chin, he looked into Alaria's blue eyes. "She is my twin flame. The other half of my soul. You know that. How can this be that I'll never see her again until the time of union?"

"We're aware of that, Atok," Alaria said. "But we do not design your soul's journey with the Great Mother or choose whom you will meet along the way. We are your guides, that is all."

Atok knew at some point, Chaska, the other half of his soul, would once more be with him. Linear time did not exist except in the third-dimensional realm. Still, it could be eons before he ever saw her again. He felt utterly defeated. "Very well, I'll take the education of becoming a guardian for a sacred site."

"Good," Alaria quickly praised. Reaching out, she touched Atok's slumped shoulder. "And do you want to keep this personality or not?"

"I do," he said. "It is a good personality for a guardian to have, do you not think?"

Adaire smiled. "It's a fine fit, son. Take time to heal now, to grieve for the loss of Chaska and your son. When you are ready, we will ask Chima, the Great Serpent Guardian, to take you beneath his wing to teach you. Once you have learned, Chima will move on to another point in the education of his soul and you will take over his position."

Disheartened, Atok nodded. "Very well." He turned and walked into the large, airy hut. The hard earth was swept clean, a table and chairs sat nearby fashioned out of local jungle tree wood. It was a pleasant hut but only loneliness ate into his heart and soul. Atok simply could not face any existence without Chaska. Why had the Great Mother decided to punish him like this?

Chapter 2

"The dream I had showed me where the next emerald sphere is located," Calen Hernandez-Manchahi said to the assembled group in the mission room, "It's in the United States."

Reno Manchahi, who sat next to his wife at the oval table, held up a diagram. "This is it: the Great Serpent Mound."

Aella Palas, mission specialist, sitting to the right of Calen, critically studied the photo. "Where is this, Reno?"

"Dayton, Ohio, is the nearest big city," he

told her. "You and Robert Cramer will fly in there. We'll have a rental car standing by for you once you get on the ground. The mound is east of the city and located on Route 73 in Adams County. There is no town located next to this sacred site."

Aella nodded, studied the larger diagram. "A snake. It's beautiful. It seems to move even though it's composed of earth and covered in grass."

Robert Cramer sat to the left of Reno Manchahi, owner of the Vesica Pisces institute near Quito, Ecuador. He gave a mirthless smile to his new partner. "You're a New Yorker, aren't you, Aella?"

Aella resented the slight derision she heard in Robert's tone. She knew she was definitely not a complete city dweller. "I'm only slightly citified," she said. Looking to Calen, she saw the woman grin. "Is my city showing?"

The people at the table broke out in collective laughter. The early-morning sunrays came through the floor-to-ceiling windows on the east side of the large mahogany-paneled room. Aella had arrived just yesterday and jet lag still dogged her heels. Still, the institute, which was becoming world famous for its online lessons regarding metaphysics, was a beautiful place with good energy. Aella liked the fact that very few people knew about this super-secret mission. Even though she hadn't warmed up to him yet Robert Cramer was very good-looking. Aella would enjoy him from afar.

"City has its place," Calen said. "You were chosen, Aella, because of your psychic background. You're fully clairvoyant and we need that on every mission to locate the next emerald sphere." She gestured to Robert, dressed in field khakis and a vest, his hat on the table beside him. He was like a young Indiana Jones. "You are the psychic bird dog, so to speak, and Robert brings not only archeological expertise but he's from a family of shape-shifters."

Robert nodded. His sleeves were rolled up to his elbows, his hands clasped in front of him on the table. "I'm not sure how much being a

shape-shifter is going to play into this assign-
ment, Calen."

"You never know," Reno said. "We like
to send out teams consisting of a man and
woman. Each brings his and her strengths to
the collective table. After three other missions
we've found that this balance is absolutely es-
sential to finding the sphere."

"I'm eager to get started," Robert confided,
smiling across the table at Aella. She was
twenty-six, six feet tall and came from Greek
heritage. Her hair was black as a raven's wing
with blue highlights, slightly curly and gathered into a ponytail at the back of her slender
neck. Robert found her beautiful and could
imagine that in the ancient era of Athens' hey-
day, she'd have been a Greek goddess come
to life. In particular, he liked her light-gold
eyes. They glimmered with such life and easy
humor. There wasn't much to dislike about
his teammate. He wondered if she was married and saw no ring on her left hand. Now-
adays, that meant nothing. On the airline trip

to Dayton, Ohio, he'd have to quiz her about her personal life—without offending her, of course.

"We're eager to get you to the mound," Reno said, opening up the file before him. "Let's get into the mission, shall we?"

Aella opened her file. There was a small photo of the serpent mound and plenty of written data to go with it. Heat tunneled up from her throat and into her face. The way Robert looked at her made her feel giddy. He was terribly handsome with a sun-darkened oval face, a strong chin and confidence to burn. Indeed, as she tucked a smile away and studied the file information, she decided he was definitely a bit arrogant and cocksure about himself. But maybe he had good reason, given his history. She knew next to nothing about shape-shifters. His energy signature was interesting to say the least and she allowed herself to feel a bit of his aura. Well, it wasn't really the time or place. They'd have enough time together.

"Calen's dream located the fourth emerald

sphere at this ancient sacred site in Ohio," Reno told them. "I've been there and it's a hot spot of psychic activity—very interesting and unique energy." He looked at the two of them. "You need to map it energetically, find out about it, what it's hooked up to, if anything. And, by being there, we are hoping that the sphere will be stimulated to show itself. As you know, the Incas created the Emerald Key necklace in the time of Emperor Pachacuti. He sent priests around the world to hide these seven hand-hewn emerald spheres. Each sphere was imbued with a particular energy. For example," Reno pulled up another photo to show them, "the first was about forgiveness. The second one was inscribed with the word *faith*. The third was trust. We have no idea what this fourth one is about. Whatever quality the sphere has inscribed on it, the team tends to experience."

"It would be nice to know what we're facing," Robert grumbled.

Calen shrugged. "I wasn't shown that information in my dream. It's as if the team has a certain karma that they must walk through in order to retrieve the orb."

Aella brightened. "It makes me wonder what my karmic education is going to be all about."

Reno frowned. "This is going to be dangerous, Aella. We don't want to make light of this. Our chief nemesis is Victor Carancho Guerra. He is the Dark Lord and chief sorcerer for the *Tupay*, the heavy energy which stops us from evolving and becoming more compassionate human beings. Heavy energy pulls us down and brings out our worst, not our best. It represents such human emotions as anger, hatred, prejudice, betrayal, disloyalty, lies, stealing, cheating and killing. Guerra nearly killed Kendra Johnson, who was on the last mission. As a sorcerer, he can invade your body and possess you."

His voice deepened. "You don't have the energy or power this man in spirit has. If he nails you, you will die when he exits your body."

Grimly, Reno looked at them. "The only reason Kendra survived was because of last-minute intervention by Grandmother Alaria and Grandfather Adaire from the Village of the Clouds. That is a fourth-dimensional stronghold for the *Taqe*, the People of the Light. That is the one place the *Tupay* cannot gain entrance. They were able to bring Kendra's spirit back and reattach it to her physical body. And that's the only reason she's alive today."

Calen nodded and shared her husband's grim warning. "We cannot always rely on Alaria or Adaire to bring back one of our possessed team members. This was, from their perspective, a one-time thing. Usually, the Laws of Karma forbid them from interceding."

"So it means if Victor is around, we have to be on our toes," Robert summed up critically.

"He will be," Calen said in a quiet tone. "You can count on it. He desperately wants to get one of these spheres. If the *Tupay* are able to get them instead of us, they can change the world's energy to heavy energy. The forces of

Light will have lost the chance to change Earth for the better. So far, Guerra has shown he's willing to kill to get any sphere."

"But why can't he find one himself?" Aella wondered.

"The spheres were created by Incan priests and priestesses who are *Taqe*. They are of the Light which promises compassion and bringing out the best in human beings. Emperor Pachacuti was told by his astrologers that between February 11, 2011, and December 21, 2012, our world, as we know it, will change. This doesn't mean the physical end of the world. Many people haven't really looked at the true Mayan inscription. It means time as we know it will no longer exist."

"Linear time?" Robert asked, curious.

"Exactly," Calen said. "We have an opportunity to move from linear time to an unknown non-time world. It's an evolution of the planet and those who live on it. Can we do it?" She opened her hands. "We don't have all the answers. But we do know that the Emerald Key necklace was created to help bring about this leap in evolutionary energy. By finding the seven emerald spheres, restringing them and allowing Ana Ridfort to wear it, we have a chance. Ana's power is from the heart and she is the only one who can do this. When and if that time comes, we can respond positively to this coming time shift that the Mayans have predicted. She is the estranged daughter of Victor Carancho, the Tupay Dark Lord."

"So, nothing is guaranteed," Robert said.

"No," Reno growled. "When we send out a team, it is not a promise that we will automatically find the sphere and bring it back. Each time is new. Each time, we could lose both of our operatives to Guerra. That's not something we want. You need to know how dangerous this is. You could die."

"And," Calen said more gently to the couple, "you need to know you can back out of this mission and not feel ashamed of doing so. This is life and death. We've chosen the two of you because of your backgrounds and skills. What

happens when you get there is going to change
moment by moment. It's going to be on your
shoulders. All we can do is sit back, pray and
hope that you are successful."

"I see," Aella murmured. She came from a
line of Greek priestesses who had served the
goddess Athena through the centuries. Athena
was her mentor, guide and protector. She was
a warrior goddess, and Aella felt secure that
her chief guide would protect her during the
coming mission.

"I'm in," Aella said.

"I feel my guardian is up to the challenge,"
Robert intoned. "I've been in many, many dangerous situations and he's never not protected
me. I'm part Native American and have been
trained to work with my guide."

Aella grimaced inwardly. Robert appeared
to be totally confident. In her growing-up years
under the tutelage of Athena, she had realized
quickly that life and death were inextricably
bound to one another. Athena, who was known
for her beautiful weaving, had shown Aella

how easy it was to lose one's body, the spirit cut free from the silver cord that tethered it to the human vehicle. No, she was not as confident as Robert. She had never seen anyone possessed. What were the signs? But then, Robert may have had many experiences in the past to make him feel so sure about everything. Still, Aella's approach was one of caution, of listening to Athena, who sent her hunches. So long as she listened to them, she would have some protection.

Calen gave her husband a tender look and then said, "Reno and I wish you the best. We're here if you need us. Just keep up daily reports to us by satellite phone. Everything you need for your journey is ready. Alberto, our driver, will take you to the Quito airport to pick up your flight to Dayton, Ohio. Good luck."

"I'm looking for a bio on you," Robert said with a casual smile. They sat in the first-class section of a Condor Airlines jet as it flew toward the USA. "I find nothing."

Aella nodded. "I guess they wanted us to get to know one another on this flight."

"Not an altogether bad idea," Robert murmured. He liked Aella's white linen suit. She looked cool and professional. It was July in the USA but in South America, below the equator, it was winter. And linen wasn't exactly warm, although Quito was hot year-round in his experience. It was then he noticed her earrings. About the diameter of a nickel and vintage, they showed. "I'm fascinated with your jewelry." He pointed a finger toward her delicate earlobe. "Tell me about these."

"They are very old," Aella said. She touched one of the earrings. "My metaphysical background is, well, interesting."

"I'm all ears."

She smiled and fixated briefly on his very male mouth that curved like a delicious dessert. "My Greek name means *whirlwind*. I come from a family with a tradition of serving Athena. I was told by my great-grandmother shortly before she died that our line of women goes back to the time of the women Amazon warriors. In the myth, Aella, who was a famous Amazon warrior, was killed by Hercules. He was trying to steal Queen Hippolyta's girdle. Aella died, but she had a daughter who continued the family line to the present. My grandmother told me I was the first girl child to be given her name."

"Do you know why?" Robert was entranced with Aella. Soft tendrils of curly black hair framed her oval face. The heat and humidity had curled them gently against her olive skin.

"No. However, my mother took me into psychic training at age nine, shortly after my grams died at our home. I missed her terribly because she was my main teacher. My training was to bring out my skills to see into the other dimensions and to talk with spirits. Because she died early, my skills weren't completed. I was never introduced to possession or what it looks like in a person's aura. In some ways, I feel less than capable on this mission."

"I think you're up to it. And I don't know anything about possession, either, so on that point, we've got a weakness. We'll just need to try and remain alert. So you talk to the dead and undead?" Robert asked.

"You could say that. My mother trained me to talk with local 'little people' or etheric beings, devas who rule over certain areas or regions and spirits who guard sacred sites."

"We'll certainly need all of that on this mission," Robert said. He watched a lovely young Ecuadorian flight attendant serve them champagne before their lunch. Picking up his champagne glass, he tipped it toward hers. "I'm glad for your sight, but tell me about those earrings."

Aella chuckled before taking a sip of her champagne and setting the glass down on her table. "These earrings are said to have been worn by the first Aella in my family. They were passed down and given to the girl child of each succeeding generation after she graduated and developed her skills." Touching them,

Aella said, "I love them. I'm never without them. They make me feel good."

"Yes, they are beautiful," Robert agreed, enjoying not only looking at the earrings, but at Aella. Her flesh was flawless, a slight tinge of pink to her cheeks. "You're a psychic bloodhound of sorts."

"I've never heard it put that way, but yes, I suppose I am."

"And what do you do for a living with all these skills in place?"

She smiled slightly. "By day I work for a charity, Children of the World. My job is to get wealthy corporations and patrons to contribute and help bring education to third-world countries."

Robert sensed Aella would be very good with children. She had that kind of nurturing and maternal energy around her. Not all women had that, but she had it in spades. "You're doing good in the world."

"My lineage insisted upon that," Aella said, grinning. "The Palas family heritage is to pull those less fortunate up out of the trenches and give them a chance for a better life. It begins and ends with education."

Robert couldn't agree more. The flight attendant refilled their champagne glasses, smiled and told them that their lunches would arrive shortly. The sound of the jet engines combined with the fine shudder that always ran through any airliner always bothered him. He was super sensitive to noise anyway. Lucky for him, Aella was a nice distraction. "I notice that even your last name, Palas, is a direct spinoff of Pallas Athena."

"Yes, in Rome she was called Minerva and in Greece, Pallas Athena. My grams said that our family name, *Palas,* was given to the daughter of the first Aella."

"You're truly a keepsake family with an incredible history. Talk about providence," he chuckled.

"Ah, the archeologist has his wolf ears up?" she teased, smiling at him. There was nothing to dislike about Robert. His personality grew on her, as did his innate charm. It didn't hurt that she loved looking at him. He was darkly tanned because he was out in the field most of the time. His skin was weathered and at thirty-four years old, he was at his peak. He wasn't overly muscled, but rather lean, like a swimmer. In particular, Aella liked his roughened, work-worn hands—square with long, almost artistic-looking fingers. But weren't archeologists the artists who could look at a land shape and know that something was hidden beneath? And with those fingers, couldn't he pull off the debris and time and age to find it? His green eyes were wide with intelligence and curiosity. The color reminded her of summer leaves on a tree.

"Absolutely. Having a lineage like that is fascinating to someone like me."

"Maybe when we get done with this mission, you'd like to visit Greece? My family lives in Athens."

Robert had other motives in mind. "That's an invite I won't pass up. Thank you."

"What about you?" Aella pressed. "Were you chosen because of your knowledge about the mound people?"

"I'm sure I was," Robert said, sipping his champagne with appreciation. Where he generally worked, there was no liquor around at all. "My forte is regarding the Fort Ancient culture in the middle of the United States. It's a culture that began around 1000 A.D. This was part of what people refer to generally as the 'mound builders,' but there were several different times and peoples who contributed to their being built."

"And how old is the Great Serpent Mound?" Aella wondered.

"Charcoal was located near the Serpent Mound and the tests results were dated around 1070 A.D. This helped archeologists who wondered about this particular site. It wasn't the Hopewell Group as every one thought. Rather, we found out it was the Fort Ancient people instead."

"And that's your area of specialty?"

"Yes." He frowned. "Actually, there are two different cultures who we believed help build that site. The Adena people lived in the Ohio area from the sixth century B.C. to the early first century, A.D. Then, you had the Fort Ancient people who arrived after that. These two cultures are the ones we feel built the serpent mound so far as we can prove right now."

"I'm anxious to get there," Aella confided, excitement in her voice. "I've never seen it in person. Only in photographs."

Robert thanked the flight attendant as she picked up their empty glasses. "You'll be enthralled," he promised her. "The mound is twelve hundred feet long and five feet high. It's made of earth and is formed in the shape of an uncoiling snake. Its mouth is open and there is an egg between its jaws."

"Can you imagine carrying dirt for that creation?" Aella mused. The flight attendant brought their plates filled with food, and Aella hungrily dug into her shrimp cocktail. She loved seafood.

Robert grinned and placed the napkin in his lap. "No, I wouldn't have wanted to be on the workforce to create that serpent. Remember back then they didn't have wheelbarrows? They'd have to carry a woven basket filled with dirt to that effigy. When you start doing the math on the time it took, you can see why it took two cultures to finish the project." He cut into his filet mignon.

"What does the serpent do? What did they use it for?"

There was nothing more sensual than watching Aella eat. Maybe it was her lips. They were full and wide and quick to turn into a beaming smile. Robert pulled his thoughts from the personal to the professional. "It's a mystery. We know it wasn't used for burial purposes. Plenty of mounds surrounding it contained graves and skeletal remains. But no graves are at the serpent. Some archeologists think it was created as an offering to the gods or goddesses of their time and belief." He wiped his mouth with the linen napkin. "What is of more interest to me is this: You can't see the serpent mound if you're on the ground. It's completely hidden by terrain, bushes and trees. Yet, if you were in the sky, you could easily spot it."

"Hmm," Aella murmured, "what does that mean to you?"

Robert shrugged. "The creative side of me ponders such things as visits by aliens from other galaxies. Flying saucers. Our culture did not have flight at that time. I postulate aliens did visit."

"I like that possibility," Aella said. She had finished her shrimp and prepared to begin on a beautifully presented salad filled with greens, grilled chicken and sliced almonds. The balsamic dressing smelled heavenly. "And the science side of you?" She liked that Robert had a fanciful side. In his career, it was more likely he'd stick to science and not wild, unsubstantiated ideas like flying saucers or alien contact.

"I've written a paper regarding the symbolic and mythological viewpoints of the mount.

The serpent's tail is coiled and that is a very common symbol seen throughout all ancient cultures. For these people of those times, the symbol represented the sacred Earth forces. My other thesis was that those cultures were possibly worshipping the Earth as their divine mother."

"And that's scientifically going out on a limb?" Aella asked, smiling.

"Yes. I've earned plenty of scientific scorn from my fellow archeologists because of that paper."

"Do you care what they think?"

"No. Symbols don't lie. Humans interpret them to the best of their ability. So far, none of my colleagues has come up with a better explanation."

Sighing, Aella said, "I'm truly excited about being there with the serpent, Robert. It sounds like it is an incredibly sacred site."

"I think it is. I like going to visit it. I always feel uplifted, cleaner and more energetic after walking the serpent, tail to head."

"We'll get to walk on it, too?"

"Oh," he chuckled, "probably more than you ever dreamed of doing."

"I work by walking," Aella told him. She picked up an almond and slipped it into her mouth. "I'm sort of like a radar detector. Where I walk, I can make contact and pick up the energies and try to figure it all out."

"That's great," Robert said, finishing off the last of his steak. "I'll just follow behind you with paper and pen."

Laughing, Aella enjoyed the teasing look in Robert's green eyes. "Your wife must hear great stories when you return from a dig."

His brows moved downward. "I was married," he told her, "but my wife, Tracy, died two years ago from breast cancer."

"I'm so sorry," Aella whispered, placing her hand momentarily on his lower arm. "You must miss her terribly."

"I do." He gestured for the flight attendant to come and remove his tray. "Tracy was my best friend. And she often used to accompany me on digs. She was an amateur archeologist, but she had the heart and soul of a professional."

Feeling his loss, Aella understood. "Two years ago I was engaged to Theo." Her voice softened. "We met in Athens. My mother liked to set me up with suitors. Theo was a medical doctor. He was such a humanitarian. He worked in the agricultural areas of Greece where there aren't many doctors. I admired his compassion for the working people."

"This doesn't sound as though it will have a happy ending."

Shaking her head, Aella whispered, "No, it doesn't. Theo was flying in a private plane back to his rural clinic when the plane crashed during a thunderstorm. He died instantly along with the pilot."

Robert saw the loss in her golden eyes. "Looks as if we've both suffered tremendous loss."

"Yes," she said. "Now, that seems like another life to me. I'll never forget Theo or his compassion."

"No one in your life now?" Robert wondered.

"No. I'm finally coming out of the shock of Theo dying. Grief has its own time and way."

"That's true for all of us," Robert said, knowing he wasn't completely over the loss of Tracy, either. Still, just being around sunny Aella, his lonely spirit lifted. And in his heart of hearts, he was interested in her not as a mission teammate, but as a woman. For the first time since Tracy's death, he felt a renewed interest in living.

Had the magic of the Great Serpent Mound been responsible? Robert knew the snake was one of the oldest symbols in the world. It was about life, death and rebirth. Would this mission bring all those things?

Chapter 3

"Do you feel that?" Aella asked Robert as they retrieved their luggage from the airport carousel. Her skin was crawling. Something didn't feel right. It was 8:00 a.m., so there were not too many people hustling around them to grab for their bags.

Robert pulled out two huge dark-green canvas suitcases and set them down. "Feel what?"

Frowning, Aella looked around. "I don't know...."

"Describe it." He grabbed her red leather

suitcase and placed it beside his own. Aella packed lightly compared to him.

As she looked around again, she sensed a dark, malevolent presence in the corner of the huge airport facility. "Something evil…"

Robert noticed her intently staring at one corner in particular. "I don't feel anything." And then he grinned. "I'm a shape-shifter, not a psychic, so you may well be picking up on something I can't feel."

Nodding, Aella picked up the T-handle on her suitcase and pulled it behind her. "Maybe I'm just tired from the long flight. My psychic apparatus isn't always on, nor is it always accurate. When I'm tired, the information I receive gets diluted and it's hard for me to interpret it with accuracy." Still, she felt something nearby and it nagged at her. Her skin became bumpy as a shiver worked through her. Something was watching them. She had no doubt.

Victor Carancho Guerra hung in the corner of the baggage-claim area just watching and evaluating the two people sent by the foundation to find the next emerald sphere. He was invisible to those in the third-dimensional world. Well, almost. He saw that the woman named Aella was a skilled clairvoyant. If she hadn't been so tired from the flight, she'd have seen him in his fourth-dimensional world. Psychics could see into that particular realm. She was sensing him, however, and that warned him about her abilities.

Smiling to himself, Victor turned to one of his trusted knights, the men he kept for protection. Lothar had been a soldier in thousands of lifetimes and was one of his most trusted advisors. The man was dressed in a wheat-colored tunic and breeches, his legs wrapped with cloth befitting his Celtic status as a warrior from 200 A.D. That had been his last life before Victor had snatched him up to serve the *Tupay*.

"What do you think of the male with her?" he asked him.

Lothar shrugged. "He's a shape-shifter. I see a cougar hanging around him. Not much to worry about, I'd say."

"I agree," Victor said telepathically. In the fourth dimension, one could utilize one's mental abilities for communication so the men didn't have to speak, although they could if they wanted to. "His aura is strong but not as strong as hers."

"Indeed," Lothar agreed. "I sense a very powerful presence around her but I cannot perceive it."

"That's right," Victor said. "Whoever it is has cloaked herself. And it is a female."

"Gods and goddesses do that," Lothar said flatly, continuing to observe the twosome.

"And if that's the case," Victor said, stroking his neatly pointed black and gray beard, "then we have to be very circumspect around her." To tangle with a god or goddess was to take on a power that made Victor wary. These iconic souls were powerful because people had worshipped them for thousands of years. The thought forms known as energy packets created by such worship made them formidable. If the god was worshipped by thousands, then those thousands of packets were exponentially bumped up in power for the owner. Pure, unadulterated power. People did not realize that every time they prayed, they created such energy. No, Victor had to find out more about the woman, Aella. Her guardian protector was very powerful—probably more so than any power he could call upon.

"The man is open compared to her," Lothar noted, gesturing toward them.

"Yes. He's more available to us. But then," he turned and looked at his friend, who wore his blond hair in two long, thick braids, "the real question is: if we go after him, will the woman or her guardian jump in to try and protect him from us?"

"We won't know until you try," Lothar said, tugging on his scraggly beard. "After all, there is karma involved. Whatever you do with the man might be within the agreement of his spirit in this lifetime."

Grunting, Victor's eyes narrowed on the tall, lean man. He was a fine human specimen: young, strong and healthy. Just what Victor preferred. Cramer wouldn't be easy to access, that was for sure, but he'd be far easier than the woman. "I wish for the millionth time we could access the Akashic Records to find out if there is karma involved or not."

"They aren't available to the *Tupay*," Lothar reminded him as always.

"I know," Victor rasped, gritting his teeth. The Akashic Records were housed in a series of buildings, somewhat Greek in structure, located in the fourth dimension. This was the repository for every person's thoughts, spoken words, actions and journey through a given life. The hall served as a focal point for the guides of a soul to decide what the next incarnational education would include. The *Taqe,* or People of the Light, had ongoing access. Those who practiced the heavy energy of the *Tupay* were barred. Victor could have found so much more information and used that knowledge as a way for the Dark Forces to win the fight over the Light. *It's not fair!* he thought angrily. He thought of the Village of the Clouds, the Warriors for the Lights' stronghold. That too was off limits. If Victor tried to enter the hall of the Akashic Records or step across that bridge into the village, he'd die instantly. The dark could not stand light and it was always destroyed by it. Such was the cosmic law that he had no control over.

Without specifics on Robert Cramer's current incarnation, Victor couldn't gauge whether possessing him would be a viable strategy. If Victor went after Cramer and his karma and education did not include being possessed, then Victor would find himself fighting for his life—quite literally. The stakes were too high to gamble. Right now, the *Taqe* had three of the seven emerald spheres. If they retrieved the rest, then his faction would lose the war and the Light would be victorious.

Balling his fist, Victor felt rage tunneling through him. That just could *not* happen! He was the Dark Lord! The person all *Tupay* looked up to. They expected him to win this latest war between Light and Dark. Victor thought about making Lothar perform the possession of Cramer, but he never trusted anyone but himself with such crucial missions. Still, if Lothar died, he wouldn't care.

As Dark Lord, it was his duty to shoulder the heavy responsibility. Victor wished once more that he was with his Peruvian family in Cusco. How he missed his beautiful, pliable young wife. He ached to see his two young children again. Oh, to be able to hold them in his arms once more! To kiss their hair, touch their angelic, innocent faces. Sometimes, the loss of his human body was too much for Victor to bear. He pushed his grief and loss aside as he studied the twosome exiting the airport facility.

"I'll wager that Cramer's karma is going to be an open door for you, sire," Lothar said.

"Maybe," Victor growled unhappily. "We *must* get this sphere, Lothar. Nothing else will do. My people are restless. They expect more of me than coming up empty-handed every time." Relaxing his fists, Victor floated through the building structure and tailed the twosome as they got their rental car. He didn't want to get too close because he knew Aella would sense him.

"My Lord," Lothar said reassuringly, "the game is about to tip our way. I'm sure we'll get the sphere this time."

Victor wasn't so sure. While Lothar was correct about tipping points of energy on such things, they were overdue for a sphere. But he couldn't count on that. If he wanted the sphere, he'd have to pursue it aggressively. "Tipping our way will happen when we power through the situation and steal the sphere. It is two mighty foes facing one another. Whoever has more power will get it."

"I agree," Lothar said equably as he floated beside his Dark Lord.

Victor could easily see the cougar chief guide in place to protect and help Robert Cramer. Everyone had a chief guide, although it could take the shape of whatever the person needed in that given lifetime. Since Cramer was part Native American, his guide, of course, would be from the natural world. As Victor watched the cougar circling Cramer, he understood the fierce animal would put up a hellish fight to protect him. Some chief guides were equal to his power—some were more powerful.

Switching his gaze to Aella, Victor knew that her invisible guardian was far more powerful. Did that mean that when he attacked Cramer, Aella's guide would get involved? That was the key. He couldn't know unless he attacked. The terrible dilemma left a bitter taste in his mouth.

"Let's follow them closely enough to tap into their talk," Victor said. "Maybe we'll find out some new things about them that will serve our purpose."

Robert rolled the two suitcases behind him and they set out. The Dayton, Ohio, airport wasn't huge in comparison to major hubs, but for its size, it was airy and had plenty of room for disembarking passengers. Outside, he could see the July morning dawning, the sun strong and the humidity high. The humid "dog days" in middle America weren't his favorite; Robert preferred the dry heat of deserts where he normally had his digs.

Aella picked up their modest Toyota Corolla from the car rental agency. The white vehicle was quickly packed with their suitcases and she opted to drive. The feeling of being watched lingered strongly with her. Before she sat in the driver's seat, Aella scanned the area. Men in business suits shuffled to their cars, but she saw nothing out of place. No one watched them. Nothing seemed covert. Rubbing the back of her neck beneath her dark hair, she frowned. Sliding in to the car, she closed the door and started it up. She wished she weren't so tired. Under ordinary circumstances, her clairvoyance would allow her to see who it was, but not now. She was exhausted from the flight and time changes.

"Looks like a typical hot, humid day coming our way," Robert said cheerfully, tossing his hat to the back seat.

"I don't like humidity, either," Aella agreed as she slowly drove out of the airport. "In Greece, especially inland, it's deliciously hot and dry. I love it that way."

"Makes two of us," he murmured, punching in the coordinates on their GPS device on the dashboard.

Aella heard the GPS speak up with a woman's voice in a British accent. She stopped and then turned left onto the freeway ramp, following the directions. "It's pretty here," she noted, gesturing to the tall trees along the green slopes of the six-lane highway.

"Ohio is a beautiful state," Robert agreed. "If you love oak, maple, buckeye, elm and tulip trees, this is the place for you. The woodlands in this state are wonderful. Great if you're a botanist."

Aella smiled. She appreciated the natural beauty of a state she'd never been in before. The sun was bright and she put on her sunglasses. "Look at all the flowers on the slopes. This place reminds me of a Garden of Eden."

"Say that this afternoon," Robert said with a smile. "We're going east and out into an area of thick woodland. The humidity is going to be ninety percent by this afternoon and the mosquitoes will be attacking."

"Which is why I brought along a long-sleeved cotton blouse," Aella said, returning his smile. She appreciated Robert's craggy profile. Clearly, he was a man who regularly challenged nature on his own terms. "You never spoke much about your shape-shifting abilities on the plane. I've never met someone who could do that. Can you tell me about yourself?"

Pleased by her desire to know about him, Robert nodded. "I'm part Cheyenne. I have a younger brother and sister. On my mother's side of the family we had a 'medicine' or skill that was brought down through each generation. My mother chose to teach me the ins and outs of shape-shifting. One child in each new generation is taught this so that it may be carried on to the next one."

"That's a wonderful way to learn," Aella

agreed. "It's very much like my family's heritage."

"Exactly," Robert said. "By the time I was twelve years old, I could shape-shift into a male cougar."

"Wow…." Aella said. "Really? I mean, from human into animal before my very eyes? In this dimension?"

Chuckling, Robert nodded. "Yes."

"Does it take a lot of your energy? Does it leave you tired afterward?"

"Yes to both questions." He smiled and enjoyed her elegant profile. To him, she looked like a Greek goddess with that broad, clean brow and patrician nose. Her best feature, however, was her sculpted mouth. He wanted to kiss Aella and find out if she tasted as good as he thought she would. For now, he pushed his lustful thoughts aside. "There's a moment where I need complete peace and quiet to trigger the transformation of my body from human to a cougar."

"And you can't if you're in a stressful situation?"

"No. My mother said that with time, maturity and age, I would be able to do that. Right now, I can't. I have to go somewhere and hide. I don't ever want someone to see me make that shape-shift."

"I don't blame you," Aella said. "People would be frightened of what they saw."

"Exactly."

"So, how do you use your shape-shifting abilities?"

He was pleased with her insight and question. "If I'm at a dig where I'm suspecting thievery at night when the crew is in their tents, I'll shape-shift and prowl the area."

"And do you find thieves?"

Smiling a little, Robert said, "I have."

"And?"

"I scare the hell out of them. Imagine seeing a cougar, which is not indigenous to your country, show up and growl in your face."

Aella chuckled and traded a quick look with him. Robert was not the type to brag about his abilities, and that made him even more desirable to her. Would they get time from this mission for a little personal downtime? Aella hoped so. "And so did these thieves who saw you as a cougar ever return?"

"Nope. I've used my ability mostly at my digs to stop the theft of valuable artifacts."

"It's a good use of your ally," she said.

"Absolutely."

Aella smiled warmly and turned onto a two-lane highway. The trees looked like soldiers at attention as they sped toward their destination. The sunlight laced through the dark-green leaves of the elms along the highway. The slats of sunshine came and went as a slight breeze tickled the leaves above them.

"I'll be glad to get a good night's sleep," Aella confided to Robert. "I'm so tired my psychic abilities are nil. I don't like when that happens. I like seeing into the other dimension, people's auras and the spirits."

"I know what you mean," he said. "You feel as though you're missing a leg, an arm and one eye."

Laughing with him, Aella reached out and touched his muscled arm. His eyes suddenly sparked with sensuality. The idea that he wanted her made her a little giddy. Too giddy. Releasing his arm, she placed her fingers around the steering wheel once more. "People with second sight or a metaphysical skill like yours are different. Not everyone would understand what we go through."

"Birds of a feather," Robert told her, grinning. His heart leaped with joy. Aella's touch had been like a butterfly whispering by, her fingernails grazing his flesh . Even now, his lower arm tingled wildly. He wanted more. The mission came first and he knew that. Still, in one tiny compartment of his heart, he wanted down time with her—away from work and the emerald sphere. He sat back and sighed, contented. What adventures awaited them at the serpent mound? It would be interesting to see the mound through Aella's clairvoyant eyes. Robert was sure she'd see things that might help them understand the sacred site as well as locate the sphere.

Chapter 4

Fox awoke with a jolt. He sat up on his straw-filled pallet, rubbed his face and looked around. His woven blanket pooled around his narrow waist. The fourth dimension mirrored the third in every way. When he became the assistant guardian to the serpent mound, he'd wanted what was familiar to him from his last earthly incarnation. That was his life as an Incan warrior in Peru.

What had he felt just now? Getting up, he padded across the hard-packed dirt floor in his bare feet and thrust open the door. Outside, he could see the green, grassy snake mound in the distance. A slight fog hung about tree level, but it was quickly burning off with the rising sun. Everything seemed quiet. It didn't feel quiet. Fox sensed perturbations of energy surrounding the sacred site and decided to investigate further.

Chima, the elder guardian who had been here since the mound had been built, was now studying at the Village of the Clouds. Because he'd fulfilled his spiritual path by learning guardianship, it was time for him to move upward and learn another metaphysical skill. Fox didn't know what Chima studied. The elder would probably tell him upon his return. When Chima graduated, Fox would become the official guardian of this site.

After slipping into his white cotton tunic, Fox put on his weapon-belt made of thick llama leather. On his feet he placed a pair of sturdy dark-brown leather sandals. Part of him dreaded any disturbance. He wanted to get

through the incarnation and onto the next, anything to bring him back to his beloved Chaska.
He had liked his last incarnation and parts of
him did not want to give up the memories of
it, including those of his wife. Even now as
he pulled on the sandals, his heart contracted
with grief. It was the one event he could not reconcile within himself. The fact he'd never see
her again was still too much for him to accept.
With a grimace, he stood up and pulled a bone
comb through the long, thick black hair that
fell around his massive shoulders. He pulled
his hair to the back of his neck and tied it.

Chaska had given him a beautifully wrought
gold and emerald necklace that Fox wore daily.
The finest goldsmith in Cusco, a young woman
who had learned the craft from her now-blind
father, had created the treasure. Chaska had
had her fashion the head of a jaguar twelve
times with small, round flawless emeralds in
between each one. Several round gold spacer
beads were then strung between each set. Fox
had never forgotten his surprise and pleasure

over receiving the gift from his wife on their first wedding anniversary.

He tied the necklace in place, and it hung around the base of his neck. Fox touched it reverently, imagining in his heart he was touching Chaska once more. This piece of jewelry was the only physical object he had left to remember his wife by. How he ached to hold her once again.... His dreams of her never left him. And Fox didn't want them to. He could recall each and every torrid lovemaking session with Chaska. At times he would go to the Akashic Records and simply review their life together over and over again. Chima didn't approve of this practice, of course. He chided Fox and told him, "Better to leave the past behind. You can never duplicate it, Fox. It is only going to cause you ongoing misery and grief."

Well, that was true, Fox decided as he stoked the coals in the center of the hut. After placing a wire grate over the fire, he put the hand-beaten metal pan of milk to heat. As the milk warmed, Fox walked to the shelves on the west wall of his thatched hut. A gold metal bowl held chocolate that he'd ground by hand. Taking it, he put several dollops of the dry powder into the warming milk. This was his daily routine: get up, take care of his toilet, dress and then sit with a mug of steaming hot chocolate laced with honey, a thick crust of bread, jungle fruit and a bowl of quinoa, a grain that grew well in Peru. Then, Fox was ready for his day as guardian of the site.

Something rankled him as he poured the mixture from the pan into a large gold mug. He had been dreaming of Chaska in his arms telling him that the priestess-doctor had pronounced her pregnant with his child, when, an energy like a tidal wave had rolled through his dream. Fox had been startled awake, unsure of what was going on.

Now he looked out the open door, which gave him a full view of the serpent mound. Fox saw nothing out of order. It would be several hours before the human guards would open up the gate to allow curious visitors entrance to the sacred site. All he had to do was watch them, read their auras and make sure they didn't damage the site in any way. Everything was quiet.

As he sipped the hot chocolate, Fox frowned. He enjoyed the sun rising and slanting through the thick woodland that surrounded the site. It reminded him of golden arms shimmering through the woods to touch the raised serpent. So, what type of energy had rolled through his area? What was that sensation? Fox felt a ripple of concern but could not put his finger on exactly what it was about. If Chima were here, the elder would certainly tell him. As it was, Fox decided he'd find out on his own. At some point, the student had to become the master.

As he stepped out of the roomy thatched hut that he'd built many years ago, Fox psychically opened himself up. By unveiling, he could sense and feel every energy in the surrounding area. He saw a faint white gauze-like energy bubble that completely encircled the sacred site. Every site in the world was protected this way because it kept out the heavy energy warriors, the *Tupay,* of the fourth dimension. On Earth, all sacred sites were off limits to the Dark Forces, which suited Fox just fine. He had his hands full with the humans who came here.

As he walked the recently mowed green lawn around the serpent, Fox found nothing out of order. In fact, the sense of peace was prevalent as it always had been. In the distance, he noticed Henry, the security guard for the state park, who opened up the gate to allow automobiles within the confines. His day began in normal fashion.

Maybe Fox imagined this disturbance. After all, he longed for a little excitement. Chima would frown at him when he mentioned that he hungered for something other than peace and quiet, rumbling that babysitting a sacred site would naturally be deadly boring to such an individual who insisted upon keeping his Inca-warrior lifetime. Fox would always grin and say nothing.

* * *

It was nearly 10:00 a.m. by linear time when Fox, who was walking the perimeter of the site, felt another wave of energy. This time, it riveted him. A sense of shock rode the wave as it passed through him. Turning, he frowned and looked toward the rectangular parking area in the distance. The lot sat next to a two-story Victorian home that served as an entrance for people to buy their tickets, eat food and buy trinkets.

He saw a white car pull in. Two people got out. His heart slammed violently in his chest. Gasping, Fox narrowed his eyes. No! It could not be! A black-haired woman emerged from the driver's side of the car.

Chaska.

Only she was dressed in twenty-first-century clothing instead of the beautiful woven cotton shifts she had worn when she was his Incan wife. Tears flooded his eyes as he stood there, transfixed. He had no doubt this was his love.

Could he be seeing things?

He floated an inch off the ground and moved quickly toward the car. As he drew close, his pounding heart felt like a drum being heavily beaten. It *was* Chaska! Oh, he could see some differences—her hair was short and slightly curly, for instance, but her face, her eyes and, most importantly, her aura, showed she was Chaska reincarnated.

Fox didn't know what to do. His mind tumbled with joy and confusion. He knew that by cosmic law, he could not approach her unless she approached him first. And even though this was his beloved dual flame, the other half of his soul, he could do nothing to let her know that. As a guardian, discretion was ultimate, and Fox must obey all the cosmic laws—or else. He trembled with happiness, watching as the woman—his Chaska—closed the door and hefted a dark-green canvas bag across her left shoulder. He felt like crying.

A part of him wanted to rush up to her, embrace and hold her. Bitterly, Fox reminded himself that he was not of her world or dimension.

He was in spirit. She was in body. So many wild, aching emotions rushed through him as he stood watching Chaska walk at the side of a very handsome man. Were they married? The thought buffeted him. Chaska had had eyes only for him in their lifetime. She never looked at another man the way she looked at him.

Fox couldn't help himself. He wanted to be closer to Chaska, to find out more about her. In her life as an Incan woman of nobility, Chaska had had many psychic gifts. She could see people's auras. Fox wondered if that ability was intact. He felt it was, because he saw the violet color surrounding her brow chakra located in the center of her forehead. It was spinning, the color moving out of the chakra and flowing into the rest of her vibrant, beautiful aura. Would she sense his presence?

Fox halted as the two walked up the steps to get their tickets. If she sensed him, what then? By cosmic law, he could never tell her about that lifetime unless she realized it for herself. In no way could he lead her to that lifetime of happiness they'd shared. Certain psychic valves located in the right hemisphere of her brain were closed. She would never progress spiritually in each new life, which was why these valves had to remain tightly closed on past incarnations.

Helpless, Fox waited for the two to emerge from the house. Chaska was beautiful. She was taller, but her face…oh, her face and those glorious golden eyes of hers were the same. Fox's mind churned over the likelihood of Chaska, in another life, looking similar to her Incan appearance. And then, he remembered what Grandmother Alaria had told him.

She had held up her hand and said, "My son, don't press this matter. Chaska is your twin flame, the other half of your soul. You are the male and she is the female. You were blessed to be able to come together in a lifetime, but normally, that does not happen. And for it to occur again, well, only the Great Mother Goddess can dictate that. You must pray to her."

And Fox did. Daily. Each night before he

drifted off to sleep in his hut, he would pray to the Mother for another opportunity to be with Chaska. He hadn't specified how. Excitedly, Fox realized that the Mother had granted his wish. Even though his prayer was general, Chaska was here! Fox would recognize Chaska's distinctive auric signature anywhere. Standing, he watched as the couple came down the steps carrying a map of the serpent mound.

All Fox could do was follow discreetly at a distance, as he did with every visitor who came here. He was a guard dog, to all purposes, but this was one time when he was going to relish the task as never before.

Fox absorbed Chaska's features. Her skin, instead of being golden and touched by the sun, was more olive-colored. How he wanted to touch her curled short hair! Would the strands be as silky as when they were together? Feeling like a starved jaguar, he focused on her soft, sensual mouth curved in a smile. The man at her side was a decent person, Fox realized. He saw the cougar walking at the man's side, his chief guardian. The man was a shape-shifter by his energy signature. Fox keyed his hearing.

"What do you think?" Robert was asking. "Do you feel anything yet?"

Aella smiled a little. "Give me a bit of time to adjust. This energy is definitely uplifting, a light and happy feeling."

Robert looked at the mound that stood in the distance. "Is that common for a site like this?" he wondered.

"Yes, it is. In Greece at all the temple sites I've visited over the years, the positive energy is the same." Aella gestured around her head. "I get a sense of protection here, too." She was receiving more impressions but couldn't sort them out with Robert asking questions. From the moment Aella had got out of the car, an incredible joy had seemed to surround her like a big, warm, fuzzy blanket. She'd never felt that sensation before at any other sacred site and couldn't determine who or what it was about. Her gift of Sight was strong, but Robert's questions distracted her. Aella longed to be off by herself to digest what she was felt, but Robert was gung-ho about reaching the mound. She wanted to just wait, watch, feel and absorb.

Placing her hand on Robert's arm, she explained how she worked and said, "Give me a few minutes alone."

"I see," Robert said. He brightened. "No problem."

"See that beautiful elm tree over there with a bench beneath it?" she said, pointing to it. "I'm going to go over there and sit down. I need to assimilate this energy, Robert. I want to take notes and jot things down."

"Very well. I'll go to the mound itself and just snoop around."

"Great idea. I'll come and join you when I'm done."

He looked at his watch. "It's 11:00 a.m. Let me buy you lunch back at the house at noon. Is that enough time alone?"

Aella nodded. "Perfect. I'll meet you there." He gave her a wink and she returned his smile.

Despite his slight arrogance about his status as a world-class archeologist, one of the few to really know about the building of this site, Aella found him intriguing.

Sitting down on the dark-green wooden bench, Aella grounded herself. She placed the journal in her lap, her hands across the leather cover and closed her eyes. Inhaling through her nose and out her mouth, she felt a distinct shift take place. This was the movement from the world around her to the unseen world of the fourth dimension. When she opened her eyes, she would be able to see into the other world that overlaid the third dimension.

Next, Aella visualized silver tree roots gently moving several times around her ankles and through a point in the center of each foot before diving deeply into Mother Earth. She was now fully anchored.

If the physical body was not properly grounded, problems could occur. Aella had learned her lesson when she was very young. She'd forgotten to ground and felt a sense of spaciness, floating and not perceiving completely in the fourth dimension. She'd felt unwell for three days afterward. She had no energy, she slept a great deal and everything in her life seemed disjointed and disconnected. Aella had never forgotten that mistake.

Opening her eyes, Aella was surprised. Shocked was more like it. Floating just above the freshly mowed lawn, about ten feet in front of her, was a man. Not just any man in spirit. Her heart leaped and pounded briefly. Aella couldn't understand her reaction to him. She'd seen spirits before. The man reminded her of a fierce warrior from South America. Possibly Incan? She wasn't sure. She took in his raw and powerful masculinity. He had a scar on his left cheek and several on his dark-brown arms. Sensing he was the spirit guardian, she switched to telepathy.

Hello, I'm Aella. Are you the guardian of this sacred site?

Fox's entire body flooded with joy. Was it conceivable that his Chaska still had the same voice as when he was with her? Closing his eyes for a moment, Fox savored her golden, husky tone as if life itself was breathing through him, igniting him, and making him feel like living once more. He struggled to put his personal pleasure aside as much as possible.

Greetings, Aella. I'm Atok Sopa, the assistant guardian to this sacred area. You may call me Fox, if you like. My Quechuan name is from my last incarnation as an Incan jaguar warrior.

Aella smiled fully. Yes, she could see that Fox was indeed all warrior. At his waist in a leather sheath he wore what appeared to be a short sword, not at all Roman-looking, the blade slightly curved. *A jaguar warrior? I have read about them in history books. I see you wear a jaguar necklace. It is beautiful....*

Fox swallowed hard. *Oh, Beloved, you gave this to me.* He unthinkingly touched the gold and emerald necklace around his neck. Because he'd shielded Aella from his thoughts, she could not hear his anguished reply. Grief and a desire to blurt out everything nearly overwhelmed him. And then Fox realized that this was his test. Chima had warned him that every student would be brutally tested at some point in their training. Chima had told him that the test would be unique to Fox, not the same test any other students was given.

So this was his test. Oh, by the Great Mother, how could he pass it? Fox stood staring at Aella, dazzled by her natural beauty, her gentle nature and her husky voice that still echoed in the chambers of his hammering heart.

Managing to shield his own inner turmoil, Fox replied, *Thank you. My beloved wife gave me this treasure on the first anniversary of our being wedded to one another.* Fox could tell her a partial truth. Her eyes went soft, that gold light so strong and beautiful.

A gift of the heart.

Yes. Truly. How can I be of service to you, Aella?

I'm here with Robert, my partner, to look for something. Maybe you can help us?

Fox winced inwardly. Was Robert her wedded partner? Fox kept his face carefully arranged. His ability to shield was one of his strengths. Aella would not be privy to his tumbling feelings or thoughts. *What are you looking for?*

A green sphere. It is part of what is known as the Emerald Key necklace. Have you heard of it? Legend says that the Emperor Pachacuti had seven emerald spheres created for the necklace, ordering its creation when his courtiers who forecast the future saw a time when the world would be on the brink. The emperor had each sphere was engraved with a positive, uplifting energy that could help those with heavy energy move into the Light instead. He had seven of his priestesses and priests travel the world to hide these spheres from the Tupay, or heavy energy forces. It is said that if all seven spheres are found and restrung, Light will come to the Earth. Robert and I serve the Light. We are told that the fourth sphere is here, at your sacred site. Are you aware of it? Aella held her breath.

A frown came to Fox's large, square face. She couldn't stop staring at him or enjoying how handsome he was. His mouth, in particular, mesmerized her. The unbidden desire to kiss him came over her and Aella was surprised by the need. On some old, unknown level, she knew his spirit. In a past life? Most likely.

Fox was stunned by the request. *I know of the Emerald Key necklace only because I served my emperor Pachacuti at the time it was created. However, I had no idea where he sent his trusted advisors to hide the spheres. I did not realize that one of the spheres is here. If it is, I have no awareness of it.*

Aella felt sad. Every time she looked at Fox, her heart felt as if it would tear out of her chest. What was that about? She had no idea, but she tried to keep on task. She was here for the sphere and nothing else. *Fox, may I stay in touch with you as we work with this*

*site? Perhaps the sphere is here but it has not
revealed itself to you or anyone else.*

Aella recalled Kendra and Nolan's quest
for the third sphere in Glastonbury at Chalice
Wells; the treasure was hidden within a five-
hundred-year-old yew tree on the property,
and no one had known about it until Kendra
came. The sphere had responded only to her.
They were chosen for the third mission by the
foundation. Was it possible that a spirit guardian would not be privy to such sacred information? Perhaps. Aella had no experience to
say one way or another. All she could do with
Robert was snoop around and hope that they
were the right people to coax the sphere out of
hiding—wherever it was.

Fox saw disappointment cross her brow.
He hated disappointing Chaska—Aella. *Of
course, I will try to be of help to you.* He
wanted nothing more than to be here with
Chaska. To absorb her ephemeral beauty, to
be in touch with her violet aura and hear her
speak once more. Chaska's voice had always

reminded him of the wind in the jungle, a sound that touched his heart.

Beaming at Fox, Aella felt her spirit lift unaccountably. When he gave her a warm smile, her whole being seemed to blossom like an opening flower. What was their connection to one another? Curiosity was strong, but Aella knew they had other matters to attend to before she gave in to her personal curiosity. In the next few days, Aella knew her life would change forever. How, she had no idea.

Chapter 5

Fox couldn't stop himself from following Aella and her partner around the sacred site. His insatiable hunger to be near her, to hear her voice, to watch her gestures, drink in her laughter, brought life roaring back into him as never before. His heart throbbed with remembrance, with the past now come to life once more.

As a twin flame, Aella represented the other half of his soul. Oh, Grandmother Alaria had counseled him on this incredible phenomenon. She'd said it was rare that the male and female parts of the same soul would ever share a lifetime together, and that if it did happen, the moment one connected with the other on the physical plane they would have eyes for no other. Fox understood how fortunate he'd been to find Chaska in that Incan lifetime. Sometimes, Alaria had told him, the two individuals might be friends or even siblings. When that occurred, they remained steadfastly close and supportive of one another throughout their entire shared lifetimes.

Now, he had been blessed by the Great Mother, Fox realized as he saw the two people stand and look at their map of the mound that rose directly in front of them.

Another perturbation in the fourth dimension caught Fox's attention. He turned toward the intrusion. Outside the protective white, gauzelike bubble of energy that kept this place off limits to *Tupay,* he saw Victor Guerra himself. Balling his fists, Fox tore his attention from Aella. He moved rapidly to the entrance and remained behind the energy barrier, glaring across it at Guerra.

The *Tupay* Dark Lord hovered about ten feet off the ground. He watched Aella and Robert intently. Instantly, Fox felt an innate desire to do battle with the murderous sorcerer. Guerra would kill for whatever reasons moved him. The sorcerer, like many of the higher-trained *Tupay*, could invade a human body, take the spirit prisoner and use it as a vehicle. What was Guerra up to?

Victor smiled mirthlessly as the guardian to the serpent mound approached. Fox was Incan by dress and attitude, a warrior. But not just any type of warrior. He wore the skin of a jaguar around his broad shoulders. The look in his chocolate-colored eyes was one of controlled hatred. There wasn't a *Taqe* in any dimension that didn't hate him. The red in the jaguar warrior's aura was considerable. The *Taqe* had chosen well, Victor decided, when they took this spirit to guard this particular site.

Which made Victor all the more curious as

to whether the guardian knew the whereabouts of the emerald sphere. *Greetings, Guardian.* Victor figured he might as well be amiable, as if his showing up here meant nothing at all. Of course, the guardian would most likely think otherwise, but he could try being nice, as taxing as it might be. The Dark Lord was used to snapping orders and having them carried out. However, this warrior spirit wasn't someone he particularly wanted to tangle with if a little diplomacy could work instead.

Fox scowled as the Dark Lord tried his best to look pleasant. But he could see the sorcerer's lurid dark-red and orange aura, which warned him of imminent foul play—as usual. Chima had given him plenty of warning about Guerra. He found it karmic that both of them came from Peru—that their last physical incarnations were in that country. What energies bound them to one another?

State your business, he snarled telepathically. Instantly, the sorcerer's face went blank with rage. Somehow, Guerra managed a twisted smile, his canines showing like the fangs of a jaguar.

I have an interest in the two people who just arrived at this site, he stated neutrally. Victor made sure the idiot guardian could not penetrating his thoughts. *I know the rules. I will not cross over to follow them onto your sacred site.*

Fox snorted violently. *Sorcerer, begone. The* Taqe *want you nowhere near any of their sacred sites on this Earth. Leave.*

Victor opened his hands in a gesture of peace. *I want no squabble with you, Guardian. I honor the cosmic law of the Great Mother never to encroach upon any sacred site surrounded by* Taqe *energy. We all respect those laws at all times.*

Fox's lips compressed as Guerra moved menacingly toward where the bubble of energy ended. While Guerra stood a good ten feet outside, it was too close. Fox's energy and strength were not commensurate to the Dark Lord's powers. He could not attack and send him running off. That was not the job of a guardian. Instead, he was to remain within the bounds of the bubble of sacred energy and maintain its protectiveness. Still Fox's warrior blood pounded through his body. He would rather kill Guerra than look at him. Of course, that was impossible. One could not kill a spirit. Only the Great Mother could deign to decide whether a soul lived or died on its course to the Light. The *Tupay* were stuck in heavy energy and went though thousands upon thousands of incarnations getting rid of jealousy, hatred, envy, murder, thievery and all the other negative human traits. In Victor's case, he'd chosen a *Tupay* path and was not interested in returning to the Light. He was trapped within the heavy energy of power and control over others.

Sometimes, Fox wondered how the Great Mother had such patience with spirits like Guerra. Clearly, he enjoyed his power and use of the heavy energy. The sorcerer would kill in the blink of an eye and never regret it.

Grandmother Alaria had told him at one time that Light could not exist without Dark on the earth plane. It was the combination that helped a particular soul develop and grow. Earth was a hard school in Fox's opinion. Why have to suffer pain in order to grow? In other places, pain was not the primary teacher, but rather love and compassion reigned supreme.

Fox held Guerra's narrowed, angry black eyes.

Farewell, Guardian. It has been pleasant conversing with you. Victor figured there was no reason to combat this jaguar warrior. He could not step into the boundary and the guardian could not step outside. A stalemate for now, but Victor had other plans. He wanted to test the guardian and find out just how much of a threat he might be to his plans. He'd have to be very careful and play by the rules of the Great Mother or this prickly guardian would savage him badly. And he had no desire to spend his energy on this jaguar warrior who bristled with protective energy.

Fox watched the Dark Lord disappear. He was probably going back to his castle where the major spiritual forces of the *Tupay* lived and plotted. Just as the *Taqe*, the People of the Light, had the Village of the Clouds, the *Tupay* had their impenetrable bastion in the fourth dimension. Fox had never seen it, but had heard plenty from Chima. Turning, he went back toward Aella and Robert who still read the map of the serpent mound.

How badly Fox wanted to rush up, embrace Aella and just say hello once more. Yet, as he stood about six feet away from them, unseen by Robert, Fox had to obey the laws. Just watching her, the way her lips moved, the gorgeous sunset-gold color of her eyes, sent his aching heart spiraling with hope.

"I think we should start in the coil of the tail," Robert said, pointing toward one end of the serpent. "Don't you?"

Aella studied the grassy lawn that rose before them. The mound was twelve hundred feet long and five feet high. If nothing else, in Aella's mind, this was a testament to the many people who built the site over decades with basket-loads of earth. They must have known that the serpent they built would have a unique energy. Already, she could feel her heart chakra opening more simply by standing near the effigy. "The coil is a good place to start."

Chuckling, Robert said, "There's some symbology in starting at the tail and working our way forward to the open mouth of this serpent."

Agreeing, Aella folded up the small map. They were allowed to walk up the grassy slope, the dew of the early morning now dried. As she moved onto the serpent, Aella felt a remarkable shift in energy. It was fast-moving, much faster than she was used to encountering. Dizziness swept across her. She stopped, hesitated and then felt Robert's hand on her arm.

"You okay?" he asked, worried.

"Yes…yes, I'm fine. I just encountered a wall of new, higher energy, is all. It's swift and powerful. Wow…" She stood only a foot up on the serpent itself, allowing her aura to adjust. "This is really something." Her elbow tingled where his roughened fingers remained. She noticed the concern in his suntanned features. Something good and solid flowed between them as he cupped her elbow. She saw it in Robert's eyes, a sudden interest, desire mixed with happiness. Yes, that was how Aella felt, as well.

"I just want to stand here for a moment," she said, planting her feet slightly apart so that she could stand on her own. Robert lowered his hand and she missed his touch. "I have experience with other sacred areas in Greece and it's the same. The energy is always far more powerful, much higher in frequency and therefore, our auras must shift to adjust."

"Sort of like standing in a swift-moving river when you're used to standing on land?" Robert wondered as he stood attentively at Aella's side.

"Exactly," she said, enthused by his understanding. He might be a shape-shifter, but

Robert easily grasped her world of sensation. "Do you feel the change?"

He nodded and looked appreciatively at the length of the serpent. "I feel a shift, but it hasn't made me dizzy. I'm aware we walked through what I'd term a veil of energy, like an invisible curtain."

Aella sensed the guardian nearby. Protection emanated from him toward her. In her experience, the guardians of other sacred areas usually left her alone, but this one did not. It wasn't upsetting to her. On the contrary, Aella felt a sense of wonderful warmth and safety with Fox's nearness. She switched to her capability of clairvoyance and saw Fox standing about ten feet away from her. "I'm going to talk to the guardian for a moment," she told Robert.

"Of course," he murmured, getting out his pen from his pocket and opening up his notebook to take notes.

Fox felt his heart open as he saw Aella lock into the fourth dimension. She smiled at him with those warm golden eyes of hers. It felt as if he were being bathed in sunlight, the warmth penetrating every inch of his spirit. Never had anything felt so good—or so right. Fox bit back his anguish—and the truth about their lives together.

Good morning again, Fox, Aella greeted him. His serious features suddenly lightened and his broad, wonderful mouth pull into a smile of welcome.

It is indeed a beautiful morning with your presence here, he admitted. She colored briefly, her cheeks pink for a moment. Just knowing that his words moved her sent his spirit soaring like a condor. Aella might not remember their connection or their love, but on some very deep, unconscious level of soul memory, she responded to him and their beautiful lifetime together.

I am stunned at the energy here. What can you tell me about it, Fox? she asked.

This mound is a major center of energy on this continent. There is a ley line that twists and moves from the farthest point of South

America all the way to the North Pole. There,
it completes a global circle, he replied.

And was this mound built on that line of
north-south energy?

Fox was pleased to see that Aella understood that the planet was wrapped in an invisible web of etheric energy. And within that
etheric body of Earth, there were north-south
and east-west highways of major connections
of energy. It was this etheric body that deter-
mined the health or illness of the planet. If
the etheric body and the ley line connections
were strong, clean and unblocked, Earth was
healthy. However, these lines of constantly
moving energy could easily be blocked by pol-
lution created by humans. Once these ley lines
were dirtied up with such debris, the Earth's
health declined and the temperature rose accordingly. *Yes, across the Earth the wise hu-*
mans of thousands of years ago were in touch
with these connections. And they were guided
to build sacred sites not only to enhance the
energy, protect it, but also keep it cleansed

so that this planet could remain in balance, he said.

And so, this serpent mound is connected to a ley line that goes to the North Pole? she asked.

Yes.

And where does it go to the south of us?

The serpent mound is the major intersection point between two great ley lines that cross the planet. You are feeling the energy and its movement on two different directions—north-south and east-west. The humans who built this were very aware that such a physical counterpart must be built in order to ground the energy completely. This way, the Earth can absorb a hundred percent of the energy into her etheric body.

Aella repeated all this information, and Robert recorded it. She was thrilled that the guardian would be so generous and educational about this site. *And you ensure that these two major ley lines are kept clean?*

Yes, that is one of my responsibilities.

Where does the energy come from? Aella wondered.

Every tree on this planet is like an antenna to absorb the cosmic energy that abounds in our universe. The trees are receptive to this energy and it runs down their trunks and into their roots. From there, the golden energy is sent to the nearest ley line. There are other lines of energy that follow the structure of the land as well. This energy from the cosmos may go to one of them. The important thing to understand is that this energy is then sent via the ley line to a major site where the lines crisscross one another. It is there that power stations convert the energy for use in Earth's etheric body.

I like the fact you use the words power station, Aella said. *So, the serpent mound is an energy station?*

Yes, a vital, important one for the health of the entire North American continent.

What about Central America? she asked.

The Aztecs and the Mayan people built pyr-

amids in certain places, especially in what is known as the Yucatan Peninsula. The ley line winds through that area. The pyramid knowledge came from Atlantis before it sank beneath the waves of the Atlantic Ocean. The people from Atlantis who survived the cataclysm fled to many parts of the world after that. Some of them landed on the Yucatan Peninsula. There, they gathered the people and started the building of the pyramids to capture and enhance the ley line energy through that region.

That's fascinating, Fox! Aella answered.

Fox felt his heart skipping beats over Aella's enthusiasm. He was happy to share his knowledge with her. It gave him great pleasure to see Aella's golden eyes grow wide with wonder. She was like his innocent young bride in that moment and it brought back sweet memories of their first nights together as married lovers. For now, he had to tuck away those delicate and fragile recollections. *Yes, it is fascinating. I never tire of working to keep the energies alive and well,* he replied.

Did Atlanteans who survived the sinking of their island come here to North America, too? Did they build these mounds?

Yes, there were survivors who washed ashore on this continent. They did not have a direct bearing on these mounds being built throughout the center of North America. Instead, they were created by the Druids from England and Europe who came across in boats. They were greeted by Native Americans all along the east coast. The nations intermarried. Eventually, their goal was to get into this particular area to build mounds to support this major ley line. The Druids worked with the people of this continent. You will find mounds built down in Mississippi, through Ohio and up into Michigan and then into Canada.

So, how did the Druids know about the energy lines? she asked.

Because the Atlanteans, who survived and fled to Europe or Britain to live, handed over their knowledge to the wise men and women who resided there. That was how the Druids were created long ago. I know in your history they are called Iron Age people, but they were far wiser than today's humans about the energy, energy junctures and how to keep this planet in harmony.

Aella smiled warmly and he was moved once more. *This is so fascinating. Robert and I are deeply grateful to you, Fox. We never expected such help. You are a wonderful being. I wish you were physical. I'd run up to you and throw my arms around you and kiss you on the cheek. You're just a very dear, dear spirit.*

Fox was jolted by her unabashed emotional enthusiasm. This was Chaska. This was how she was: at once a woman but then, the wondrous, innocent child who saw life through such awestruck eyes. Tears jammed into his eyes. Quickly, he blinked them away and made sure that his raw emotions could not be read. At all costs, he must guard against such a release. She would not understand it and he could not tell her why. Bitterly, Fox swallowed before finding his voice once more.

Aella, you could repay me in a small way if you'd wanted, he said.

Oh? How? Just tell me, Fox. I'd love to do something for you in return.

It was so hard to try and remain immune to her bubbling enthusiasm. It hurt to look at the rapture in her face, those exquisite gold eyes. Her mouth, her lovely, sensuous mouth, beckoned him and made him want to be in physical body once more to love her until she fainted from pleasure. Oh, to have a human body! Fox had not wanted one since he'd graduated to the new level of spiritual development. But now, he hungered for it. He understood the trial and test before him. Chima had warned him it would come. And here it was. Swallowing hard, he whispered, *Give me permission to send you dreams. I cannot do it unless you tell me yes.*

Dreams? Why, of course! I'd love to continue our conversations in the dream state. Thank you, Fox. Your generosity is gratefully received.

With her permission, Fox would connect with her in a way that would not break the cosmic laws. But he had to be careful. Very careful. Excited by the possibilities, Fox smiled. *I will visit you tonight as you lie sleeping, beautiful Aella.* Fox could send his dreams to her no matter where she was in the world. He did not have to leave his sacred site. Dream energy was fourth-dimensional and therefore, not linear-based at all. A sudden joy suffused him, and he felt like a man who has just seen the door to his prison crack open to freedom.

Chapter 6

It didn't take Aella long to get to sleep that evening. She had a glorious warm bath and then snuggled beneath the sheets and immediately fell asleep. The dream that Fox had promised came in the early morning hours....

"Chaska! There you are!"

Chaska was out of breath and standing on the last terrace where potatoes were growing. Above her was the towering Machu Picchu, the Old Mountain. Thousands of workers were busy constructing a maze of temples and living quarters. Pushing her hair out of her face, she smiled as her mother, Suyay, hurried down the side path that led to the many stone terraces.

"Why did you leave the hut?" Suyay demanded. She knelt down in front of her eight-year-old daughter who was clearly breathless, her cheeks reddened from exertion. To her left, the workers carefully pulled weeds among the thousands of plants on the terraces. Above her, the silent fingers of the clouds that always seemed like moving breath around the mountains crossed above them. Her daughter, who had the golden eyes of a jaguar, smoothed out her spotted mud-cotton shift that hung to her spindly knees.

"Daughter, what have you been up to? I called and called for you after your grandmother couldn't find you."

Smiling, Chaska pointed to the nearby wall of jungle at the end of the terraces. "Mama, I found a blue butterfly! A blue one! Oh, you know how much I love them! I was sitting on the end of that terrace and it flew out of the jungle toward me." She beamed with pride as her mother pushed strands of hair away from her daughter's face to tie them back with a leather thong.

"Oh no, you and your blue butterflies," Suyay muttered. Determinedly, she grasp her daughter's thin shoulders. "Chaska! You must not run off like this! You must tell me or your grandmother where you want to go. This mountain is treacherous. The workers are still clearing the jungle away from it and who knows what lives in there? Just yesterday evening, a guard saw a jaguar at the edge of it. And you want to chase blue butterflies!"

Pouting, Chaska hung her head. "But, Mama, I know there wouldn't be blue butterflies around if the jaguar were awake and looking to eat. Wherever a jaguar goes, the jungle is quiet and nothing moves. If butterflies are around, I know the cat isn't nearby."

Suyay gripped her hand. "Come, Chaska. I forbid you to go near the jungle again. I don't care if there are beautiful blue butterflies in there. I don't want you eaten by a jaguar!"

Chastised, she hurried along at her mother's side. Chaska was of nobility, a niece to a princess in their Incan line. And she was thrilled to have been invited by the emperor to move to Macchu Picchu for the winter months. Emperor Pachacuti was tired of the cold, dry winters in Cusco, the central Incan city that sat very high in the Andes. Instead, he longed for the warmth of the jungle. He had sent out his high priestess of the Moon Temple to find a warmer place. She had located this wonderful trio of smooth, loaf-shaped mountains whose steep slopes were covered with thousands of orchids. This became his new winter residence.

"I held a blue butterfly, Mama. I was barely inside the jungle when I saw it flying around. I called to it and it came to me. I stretched out my fingers." She showed her right hand to her mother and wriggled her fingers. "The butterfly came and landed on my fingers! She tickled me." Chaska giggled with excitement over the remembrance. "The butterfly's legs were long and black and felt so wonderful."

Raising a dark, thin brow, Suyay said grudgingly, "Tell that to your grandmother. She will be thrilled to hear of your misadventures. When she was young, she could call bees to her. She always found honey. Did you know that?" Suyay stepped onto the last carved stone step from the gardens onto the top of the massive temple area. Straight ahead, she saw the gray rock Lunar Temple. Above it was the hitching post of the Sun. White-robed priests walked in a procession.

"I remember Grandma calling the bees," Chaska said, halting at her mother's side and watching a group of young boys about ten years old being led by singing and chanting priests. Behind them, the priestesses beat the drums that sounded like thunder throughout the complex. "What are they doing, Mama?"

"Those are the young boys in training to some day become jaguar warriors." Her voice turned grim. "That is, if they survive the tests."

Chaska had glimpsed this group of ten boys only once before in the six months since they'd arrived at Macchu Picchu. Jaguar warriors were the finest and bravest of all of the emperor's guards. They could see into the night with their clairvoyant sight. Each boy, she knew, had been chosen at birth by the Priestess of Sight. She would proclaim a boy child from a good Incan family to possess certain clairvoyant skills. The chosen family willingly gave their infant son to the emperor's Priests of the Sun. It was a high honor to be chosen, but about three-fourths of them would die at some point before they passed the final, grueling test at age eighteen. Those who survived were treated like demigods by the Incan population. They served and protected the emperor at all costs and would willingly stand in front of him to take a mace or spear. Further, the emperor trusted his jaguar warriors above all others because they had taken an oath to give their life to him. He would send one or two of them out to reconnoiter a part of the large Incan empire and they would come back with vital information.

Admiringly, Chaska said, "Mama, look at that boy. The third one behind the old priest."

Suyay squinted. "What about him?"

"I like him."

Suyay teased, "Now how could you know that? These young warriors in training are never allowed to walk among us. They live in a cave beneath this mountaintop. They are fed only by priests." These boys were trained brutally and Suyay was glad she had had a daughter, not a son. Her family line also possessed the vaunted Sight, but she was thankful that no one looked at little girls as warrior material. If Chaska wanted to become a priestess, that would befit her noble daughter. Of course, she wanted Chaska to be happy and often felt her daughter would be excellent marriage material because of her station and noble heritage. Suyay dreamed of her daughter marrying a prince; that would lift her family even higher in status.

Sticking out her lower lip, Chaska followed the procession far above them. The temple complex was on the highest part of the Old Mountain. Below it was a verdant, rectangular plaza where soldiers marched, ceremonies were held and children played. They stood just on the edge of the mountain overlooking the thirty terraces below them that fed this population of nearly one thousand people. "I just know I like him!" Besides, Chaska had seen him once before. By accident she'd chased a blue butterfly around near the entrance to the jaguar warrior training cave. A priest had caught her before she'd mistakenly entered the off-limits area.

"I saw him, Mama. He was wearing a beautiful jaguar pelt across his shoulders. He saw me chasing the butterfly and stared from behind the priest. I liked his smile! His eyes were like dark pools with moonlight splashed in them. Besides, he was so tall and strong and was so much more handsome than the other boys with him!"

"Daughter, you are headstrong and wise beyond your years." Sayay chuckled.

"Do you see him, Mama?"

"Indeed I do," she murmured.

"Does he not stand out from the rest? He's stronger and bigger than the other boys. I like the way he walks. He acts as if he is already a warrior to our emperor!"

That was true, Sayay decided. "I wonder who he is?"

"I asked Grandma after I'd seen him near the jaguar-cave training area. She said the boys come from around the empire and there's no way of knowing their names. It's such a mystery!"

"You're only eight, darling child. Marriage cannot be arranged until you are twelve. And you know that jaguar trainees don't even graduate until they are eighteen. If they survive that long."

"Oh," Chaska said primly, "I know he will survive! He's strong. I love the way he walks with such pride, as if he were the jaguar already."

"Mmm," Suyay said. She turned and ran her fingers through her daughter's long, silky black ponytail. This morning was less humid than usual and her hair was not as frizzy as it could get. "And what if your father and I prefer another boy for you at age twelve when you can become betrothed?" she teased. Chaska's golden eyes rounded.

"Mama! You promised me I could do what I wanted with my life."

"So I did."

"I want *him!*" and she shot her index finger upward at the procession that was entering the temple of the Sun.

"What if he does not want you? Jaguar warriors are special, Chaska. They don't have to marry. Many do not. They are married, in a way, to the emperor and his family."

"No, Mama. He will marry me. I know he will!" Chaska said stubbornly.

"I see…" Suyay knew her daughter's Sight was strong. Why should she argue? She had met her own husband, Cusi, when he was eleven years old. His family and her own had lived in Cusco only doors apart. It was her mother, Chaska's grandmother, Ima Sumac, who had seen the connection between them. Suyay had known then that one day, she would marry her beloved Cusi. And at age twelve, they were betrothed to one another and married at age sixteen.

"And have you seen this boy in your dreams?" she wondered.

"I have, Mama. He is my husband-to-be." She twisted a look up at Suyay. "You will not give me away to anyone else? I will wait for him." Smiling Chaska touched her flat chest beneath the colorful condor embroidered across the top of her cotton shift.

Suyay gathered her daughter into her arms and walked along the street of stone houses with thatched roofs. "Come, you need to change shifts. You've muddied this one and Grandma will not allow you outdoors again without a clean one. What would the Empress say if she saw you this muddy? She would think you a lowly worker or slave. You don't want to be unseemly. After all," she said as she walked down the hard-packed earth path, "if you think you're going to marry a jaguar warrior, you must conduct yourself with great nobility."

"I *am* noble!" Chaska said, her arms around her mother's slender neck. She waved to several children playing with a hard rubber ball between the stone buildings. They waved back and called to her to join them.

"Nobility is more than a title," Suyay reminded her daughter gently, setting her down on the porch of their home. "You must wear clean clothes, keep your hair combed and plaited."

Chaska pushed the wooden door which swung open on its leather hinges. The odor of llama meat cooking in a stew of onions and potatoes made her mouth water. Her grandmother sat beside the open hearth stirring the stew with a long wooden spoon. "I suppose noble girls do not chase butterflies?" she demanded archly.

Laughing, Suyay closed the door. "Well, let's just say that a young noblewoman shouldn't get caught doing such a thing."

Smiling, Chaska said, "Good! Because I want another blue butterfly to land on my hand."

As Suyay removed her daughter's soiled dress, Grandmother Ima Sumac unfolded a clean shift from a stack of clothes sitting on a shelf.

Chaska excitedly told her grandmother about the butterfly. Ima Sumac was in her forties, her hair long and gray with streaks of black. She was short and fat and she had arthritis in her feet, which prevented her from walking much. Chaska fiercely loved her grandmother, who cooked for the family.

"Butterflies and young men," Im Sumac clucked, pulling the shift over her granddaughter's head and straightening it out. The embroidery she had sewn on this one was Chaska's favorite: a blue butterfly. It was appropriate for the child's adventures of this morning.

Chaska smoothed the cotton shift across her thin body. She wore nothing on her muddy feet. Her mother ordered her over to a stool where she placed a large wooden bowl of warmed water so she could wash them.

"Grandma, is it true?"

"What?" Im Sumac asked, hobbling on her painful feet back to the hearth where she could sit on her stool.

"That the boy who is going to be a jaguar

warrior will look kindly upon me if I'm clean? And my hair plaited." She touched the long, unruly black hair about her shoulders.

Tittering, Im Sumac traded a look with her daughter. "Jaguar warriors are considered higher than nobility, Chaska. They are the emperor's finest spiritual warriors. They have their choice of any woman in the empire if they wish to marry." She waved a short, blunt finger at Chaska as she dipped the cloth into the wooden bowl her own feet were now in. "If you want to catch the eye of such a man, you must be clean, beautiful and conduct yourself with grace."

"Which means," Suyay said, kneeling at her daughter's feet to dry them off, "no more chasing blue butterflies."

Pouting, Chaska watched as her mother gently dried her clean feet. "I know he will love me because I *do* chase blue butterflies!"

Aella awoke slowly, the remnants of the dream leaving her feeling warm and loving. She lay in bed, eyes closed so that she could savor the family scene. Aella ran her fingers across her belly. She had felt herself to be Chaska, the little girl. The fragrance of the stew her grandmother had made still lingered.

Where did dreams end and begin? Aella snuggled into the pillow and sighed. Sometimes she dreamed of past lives. She knew she did. And at other times, it was her subconscious talking to her in dream symbols and situations. This one had felt as if it were a dream of a past life in Peru. Her mind was still fuzzy with sleep; she lingered on the periphery between the dream and this lifetime.

More than anything else, Aella remembered that young boy who strode so confidently and boldly in the group of jaguar warrior students. Somehow, she knew him. But how? Searching her awakening memory, Aella wondered if she'd met him in this lifetime. If so, from where? In her travels, she met many company types, very successful businessmen who owned their own corporations. But none of them looked like this young Incan boy.

His face was so serious, so focused. His mouth was wide and his upper and lower lip of equal size. And his long black hair lay between his shoulder blades, those shoulders thrown back with pride. His face was square with high cheekbones, his skin copper-colored. Aella remembered seeing him up close on that one occasion in the dream. He had chocolate-colored eyes and indeed they did look like deep pools with moonlight shining from deep within. His eyes were haunting, slightly tilted, giving him the look of a jaguar.

Maybe that was it, Aella decided as she moved and pulled the sheet up and over her shoulders. It was those hypnotic eyes. In a way, the unknown lad had mesmerized her in the dream. Aella could still feel the depth of his focus upon her.

When their eyes had met for the first and only time in that dream, Aella had felt a shift so deep within her she couldn't name where it connected. The feeling was one of absolute and unparalleled joy, as if seeing him had opened up her world for the first time. How could that be? Opening her eyes, Aella saw that dawn was peeking around the edges of the window curtain of her motel room.

The expression in the unknown boy's eyes touched her where no one had ever touched her. Oh, she'd had a few serious relationships with men, but this dream underscored how flimsy they had been compared to the intensity of falling in love with the boy. The emotional charge in the dream left her wanting more. Had the boy graduated from the jaguar schooling? Or had he died trying? Somehow, Aella's knew, this lad had passed all his tests and he had gone on to become a powerful jaguar warrior.

Her mind gyrated to Atok Sopa. He was a jaguar warrior, a spirit guardian now. And he had said he would send her a dream. Now, Aella had a hundred questions to ask him. What did this dream mean? Was she the headstrong and unbridled Chaska? She loved the little girl in the dream, for she had elements that reminded Aella of herself in this lifetime.

Aella pulled off the sheet and swung her feet to the cool pine floor. She wanted to speak to the guardian. First, she had to shower, wash her hair and get ready for the day. As she undressed in the bathroom, she felt torn. Her attraction to Robert wasn't as appealing or intimate as the connection she'd felt in the dream. Until that dream, Aella had had no idea how lonely she was. Not just lonely for any man—for this young boy who had made her heart stutter with unparalleled happiness. How could that be?

First, she would have breakfast with Robert and go over the day's agenda. Then, she'd angle some free time to call Fox to her. Sensing that the spirit guardian would have answers for her, Aella found herself wishing on an immature level that she could just wave off Robert and the mission and go to Fox instead.

Aella turned on the shower and closed the bathroom door. She stood naked, fingers testing the streams of water until it was just the right temperature. After stepping into the stall, she pulled the dark-green curtain closed. A bar of lemon-scented soap smelled heavenly as she lathered it against the white cotton washcloth.

Once finished, she climbed out of the shower and dried off. She pulled on a dark-pink T-shirt and a pair of form-fitting jeans. After adding a narrow leather belt, white socks and comfortable tennis shoes, she brushed her hair and looked at herself in the mirror. Aella studied her eyes. Everyone said they were beautiful. Chaska had the very same eyes and, Aella realized, the same shape of face. Now more than ever sure that the dream was really about another of her lifetimes, Aella tried to quell her excitement. Putting on the Athena earrings and a simple gold chain around her throat, Aella was ready for the day's activities.

The sun was up and shining brightly into her face as she opened the door. Down the way, she saw Robert waiting for her. There was a small restaurant nearby and she could smell bacon frying. Mouth watering, Aella realized she was hungry. Locking the door, she turned, gave Robert a warm good-morning smile and walked toward him.

"Have a good night?" Robert asked, falling into step with her as they headed for the restaurant.

"Very. How about you?"

Shrugging, Robert said, "Nightmares."

"Oh?"

"Yeah," he grumbled. "I kept seeing this bearded dude with red glowing eyes telling me he was going to kill me."

Frowning, Aella sensed his worry. "I'm sorry. Do you get these nightmares often?"

"Never. That's what's so upsetting about it," he said. Halting, he opened the door to the restaurant. The odor of freshly perked coffee and bacon frying wafted past them.

"I've felt a very dark, negative presence around here," Aella told him. A waitress directed them to a red leather U-shaped booth. As they seated themselves in it, she continued, "Maybe you're picking up on it, too? As a shape-shifter, do you sense things like this?"

"I do," he said, thanking the blond waitress for the cup of coffee she handed him. "But not to the degree that you do." He managed a smile. "How about you? Good dreams last night?"

Taking her coffee, Aella poured in some cream and slowly stirred it. "Very nice dreams."

"Tell me about them."

Aella hesitated. "I keep a journal of my dreams, Robert. I was taught by my parents never to divulge them for fear they would lose their impact on me."

Robert chuckled as he sipped his coffee and looked over the menu. "Frankly, I'd like to get rid of mine and the impact they had on me."

Seeing that he was genuinely upset over the nightmares, Aella felt a riffle of fear. The sweet joy of her own dream evaporated before Robert's nightmare. Aella decided to table her own personal desires and pay attention. Robert, she was sure, was picking up on the same entity she'd previously sensed outside the serpent mound. Was this a warning?

Chapter 7

As she and Robert walked to the serpent mound, Aella could hardly contain her need to talk with Fox. The morning was clear with a bit of haze, typical of the humid dog days of July. The site had no visitors yet—just her and Robert, who was at her side with his notebook and pen at the ready.

"What do you want to do first?" he asked as they approached the five-foot-high mound near the coiled tail.

"I want to meditate near the tail and get in

touch with the guardian." It was a selfish decision, Aella realized. She didn't want to discuss the emerald sphere with Fox, but Robert would never know that. Her questions would take less than an hour of their day. She was allowed some free time to pursue her own endeavors. The guilt bit at her conscience, but not enough to stop her.

"Okay," Robert murmured, looking around. "I'm going to go through the museum's archives and work online."

Aella smiled. "Online you'll probably get woo-woo stuff."

He grinned a little and nodded. "Possibly. I've found that there's always a grain of truth in woo-woo."

"I'll meet you at the museum in about an hour?" she suggested.

Robert settled the Indiana Jones hat on his head, pulling the brim a little lower. "Sounds good. Have fun."

She would. Aella felt a weight lift from her shoulders as she hurried around to the end of the mound. They were not allowed to stand in the coil for too many human feet would eventually destroy the serpent. Instead, she found a lovely elm tree not far from the tail of the serpent, sat down and leaned up against it. Grounding herself, Aella opened herself up to the fourth dimension. In her third eye, she saw Fox standing about five feet away from her.

He was dressed as before: as a jaguar warrior, the skin of a gold-and-black spotted jaguar across his massive shoulders. His chest was bare and powerful. He wore a black cotton skirt that fell to just above his knees, with a leather belt and a sword in a scabbard. Her heart beat a little faster. Recognizing his chocolate eyes with the splash of moon she blurted out telepathically, *I had a dream last night, Fox. Did you send it to me?*

I did. Fox saw the hope flare in her lovely golden eyes. By every Incan god and goddess, he wanted to take her into his arms, kiss her lids gently closed then trail his lips slowly down the slope of her cheek to her soft, inviting mouth.

I'm confused, she said. *I saw a little boy who was in training to become a jaguar warrior. Was that you? Because his eyes and your eyes are the same.*

Fox allowed a slight smile to pull at his mouth. By cosmic law he could not tell Aella anything. But if she asked, he was bound to tell the truth. This would not break the law. He'd hoped when he'd sent her the dream that she would ask the right questions and he could forge a connection to her in this lifetime. *Yes, that was me.*

Then...Chaska...who is she?

Fox could not tell her. That was forbidden. Instead, he teased lightly, *Who do you think she was?*

Well, her gold eyes caught my attention. Aella pointed to her closed ones. *Her eyes and my eyes are the same. Not many people have these eyes, Fox. I woke up this morning won-*

dering if I was Chaska in a past life in Peru. Was I?

His heart pounded briefly in his chest. Fox now had an open door from that life to this one. *Yes, you were Chaska in that lifetime.*

Aella's pulse fluttered for a moment as she considered Fox's answers. She felt an incredible rush of happiness that suffused her unbidden, like a tidal wave. *Then...was Chaska right? Did she marry you?* Aella held her breath. So much of her wanted the answer to be yes. But then, what would happen? Fox was in spirit. She was in a third-dimensional physical body. A lost love? Somehow, Aella didn't want to hear the answers—she knew they would be devastating to her.

Fox saw the mixture of emotions on her very readable face. The colors in her aura changed sharply, the intensity of them coming and going. He tried to shield her from his own roiling emotions. *Yes, I married you as soon as I graduated from the jaguar warrior training.* A lump formed in his throat. Tears came to his eyes that he rapidly blinked away. *You were my beloved wife, Chaska.*

A sheet of warm, thrilling energy overwhelmed Aella. She sat absorbing the unexpected wave like a thirsty sponge. In those moments, she realized that a door from their mutual past had once more, been thrown open. As she absorbed his love, his undying love that had never been destroyed, Aella realized that Fox had been much more than just a husband to her in one of her incarnations. She absently touched her heart. speeding wildly in her breast. *I don't understand why I'm feeling this way, Fox. I know we loved one another— deeply. But what I'm experiencing is...well... overwhelming to me. What is happening?* She asked a little breathlessly.

Breathe, Aella. Just breathe deeply and evenly. It will pass. Because we have connected with one another once more, all the love that we held for one another has been unlocked and is now flowing back into you. If a person connects with a past life as you are doing presently, there is a momentary sense of being overwhelmed. In a few minutes, it will ease, much like the tide of the ocean receding from the beach. Fox watched Aella blush as the energy poured back into her. Many memories would come back to Aella now. The psychic valve that had kept back all this information and these feelings had been opened. For a moment, he wondered if he'd done the right thing for the right reasons. After all, he could never love Aella.

They were a dimension apart. Did Aella's knowledge of their union help her in her present incarnation? Fox didn't want to look too closely at that question. What he'd done was not wrong, but it certainly manipulated the cosmic energy for his own desire. As a guardian, he was supposed to be above such things, for desire was a human emotion. And desire could get anyone in trouble regardless of the dimension.

Fox wondered if he'd just complicated Aella's life. Sometimes, a person who tapped into one of their past lives, found living in the present again a misery. They might want to go back to that past incarnation once more. Of course, that could happen because in the fourth dimension, time was nonexistent. And if Aella were in spirit, well, they could return to that lifetime and live it over and over again. However, the ending would always be the same, and Fox didn't want Chaska to die in childbirth again. He would not make her suffer such a fate. Even with his love for her, as self-ish and overwhelming as it was, he could not torture her beautiful spirit.

As Fox stood watching Aella's aura glow brightly, he understood that their connection would remain platonic. Oh, he could visit her in dreams, make love to her in them, but that was all. Spirits could not physically consum-mate their love. Fox missed the rapture of physical contact. While making love in dreams was satisfying, it was far from the passion of two physical bodies mating wildly with one another. There simply was nothing like it.

Aella felt the energy begin to recede, just as

Fox had promised. She watched him through new eyes. He'd been her husband. A man of great power with great tenderness toward her, yet a fierce combatant for an emperor whom he had sworn to protect with his life. Her fingers curved to her throat. *This…this is incredible, Fox.*

Yes, it was a beautiful lifetime together.

Aella swallowed hard. *I died in childbirth. That was awful. I lost our baby….*

Beloved, do not grieve over this. It was many lifetimes ago. That baby's spirit moved on and went into another incarnation, just as we did, he replied.

But you didn't, Fox. After you died in battle you were given a choice. Now I understand why you are here. You volunteered to learn how to be a sacred-site guardian. That is a well-deserved move on your soul's path.

It is. I missed you, Aella. I missed what we had. And looking back on my decision, I was still grieving over your loss and that of our child, Fox couldn't help confiding.

It sounds as if you regret your choice.

I didn't until I saw you again. Aella's face reddened once more. She looked incredibly haunting when she flushed like that. Chaska had done the same thing.

But you can't undo what's been done, Fox. You're in spirit. I'm in a body in this incarnation. I haven't come as far as you have spiritually, which is why I'm still having human lifetimes.

Fox felt her mirth and laughter. She seemed to be settling in and accepting their relationship. Worried that Aella might have problems with that old knowledge and try to continue to live in this lifetime, he said, *Your soul is bright and pure, Aella. I found out through Chima, the guardian who has trained me, that you too had a choice. You could have moved into spirit as I did, but you chose to remain on Earth to help others. That is a fine choice, too. I don't know many souls who would come back when they did not have to.*

Well, Aella laughed, *that sounds like something I'd do. I love Earth. She is a beautiful planet and so many people struggle down here. I feel that if I can lift a bit of the heavy energy and transform it into Light energy, then it was worth my incarnations.*

It is just like you to do that. You were loved by everyone on Machu Picchu. Your bright light, your heart, touched everyone in a positive way. How Fox wished he could have that back. They stood at a new juncture with one another. Aella seemed to pick up on those thoughts.

What now, Fox? What is our relationship today?

What do you want it to be? I know what I would like, but I will not force my need upon you because you have this incarnation and have a plan on how to live it.

Aella could feel Fox protecting her from his feelings. She saw the shield he'd placed around himself. Was it to protect her? Did he not want to influence her regarding a connection with him? What *did* she want? Feeling the bark of the tree against her back, she tried to think clearly. Each incarnation had a road map of experiences and lessons a soul wanted to learn apart from those learned in past lives. Now, she had opened Pandora's box. Her heart twisted in her chest like a living thing. The heated awareness that she'd loved Fox with every breath in her body made it tough to think at all.

Can you answer me this, Fox? Why do I feel as I do toward you? I've never had this type of love for any man in this lifetime of mine. Oh, I've been in love before, but this is so different that I don't know what it's about.

Fox sighed, maintaining rigid control over his own feelings. *Have you heard the terms* twin souls *or* twin flames?

Yes, she replied.

When a soul goes out to learn through experiences in all dimensions, it splits itself apart into female and male components. When the soul's two pieces meet in a given incarnation, a profound depth of love is generated. It is the union of the soul once more. Usually, once the soul splits itself apart, it only comes together at the end of learning and it is ready to return to the Great Mother. And when it occurs in a physical lifetime, then it is the ultimate of love between the two people.

I see. Our Incan life was very special, a rare thing.

Yes. I wish it wasn't…

Aella grimaced. Her feelings were in an uproar. The desire to run to Fox, to embrace, kiss and love him to renew what they had had in Peru, was powerful. Yet, she couldn't go there. *If we were meant to get together in a lifetime, then you wouldn't be in spirit, Fox.*

Yes, I believe that to be true. But, here you are. You came to me. I know you're searching for the emerald sphere, but I happened to be the guardian here. There is some Fate here, do you not think?

Nothing happens by accident. But it's a hell of an accident, Fox. We can't have one another as much as I wish it.

His heart wrenched in his chest. Fox felt as if he had just been struck with a mace. The explosive pain radiated throughout his body.

Aella was thinking much more clearly than he. Fox admired her for that, for he was far weaker than she in this objective perspective. *We could be friends.*

That would be wonderful. But I have to try and focus on this life, Fox. I don't want to now that I know what we shared, what is alive within me....

Feeling guilty, Fox frowned. *I'm sorry if this is upsetting to you, Aella. I only meant to reconnect with you in some way.*

Aella felt his desperation, his absolute and undying love for her. She sensed Fox's frustration over being in spirit. Indeed, he ached to be in a physical body. That was impossible, of course. Still, Aella wondered what she would do if he were here. There was no question of the love pulsating wildly and deeply between them. No man she met from now on could ever stack up to Fox. They were the two halves of one soul. And they'd been blessed to have one lifetime together as man and woman.

This is a lot to digest, Fox. I need time to

feel my way through it. Aella sighed in frustration.

Of course you do. I will not bother you again unless you call me, Aella. And I will not send you any more dreams.

Aella was bereft. Fox was doing the right thing: he was backing off to give her room to adjust. And yet, she was desperate to have Fox as close to her as possible. This was a terrible dilemma for her. Her spirit yearned for Fox. Just to have him near was all she wanted. To think of him leaving her tore at her spirit.

Fox, can you feel my emotions right now? She asked.

Yes, I can. That is the beauty of being twin flames. We are in constant touch with one another.

Do you feel as I'm feeling right now?

Yes. I have been in this emotional state of longing for you since I died and passed into spirit. Fox regretted his foolish decision to send her the dream. *I was wrong to initiate this connection. I see that now. I didn't want you to feel pain and loss, Aella. Only my love for you. I didn't think clearly enough to realize that you would now carry the same longing and need.*

Unconsciously, Aella rubbed the area over her heart. *This makes me feel more alive than I have ever been, Fox.*

Fox felt as Aella did. *I know, Beloved. I hope that someday we can meet in another lifetime and share the joy and bliss we had in Peru.*

There was such bitter sweetness to his words. To feel this depth of love, this voracious hunger to be in each other's arms…and it could not happen. *I've just been given a prison sentence. I can love you from afar but I can't have you.*

I know…. Fox experienced firsthand the culmination of his tactics. And now, he understood why the law had been created. Feeling Aella's misery, he took upon himself the blame for it. If he truly loved her, he would not have done what he did. Fox uttered a curse in Quechua.

And Aella would live the rest of this incarnation trapped by another lifetime intruding on this one. He'd triggered it with his own selfishness. He'd completely failed this test. And he'd hurt the woman he loved most in the world.

Aella, you must try to put what we have behind you. It is best that I remain here. You must search for the sphere, but once you leave, it must be forever. That way, you can focus on this lifetime.

She heard his desperately spoken words. Opening her eyes, she broke the connection to Fox.

Robert emerged from the museum and headed in her direction. Looking at her watch, she realized she'd been talking to Fox for two hours. She rose, dusted off her pants and walked around the end of the mound to meet Robert. Her heart was anguished. This was a special hell she'd just entered. Aella had heard her grandmother tell her many times that it was not good to know about one's past lifetime, for they would stain the present one.

She did indeed feel stained, blessed, cursed and joyous. Her range of emotions both illuminated and darkened her spirit. As she waved to Robert, Aella realized she would have to learn how to live two lives at once. It seemed impossible. She was contracted to find the emerald sphere, and she was allowing her personal life to intrude upon the mission. That couldn't be. She must refocus at all costs.

As Robert closed the distance between them, Aella's eyes met his. He was a true man of the outdoor world, of adventure. There was nothing to dislike about him.

"Hey, I got some fascinating info," he said to her as he drew close. Opening his notebook, he turned it around for her to look at. "Check this out, Aella."

Aella concentrated. Her hands closed over Robert's and she studied his notes. "Wow. Caves? Around here?"

"What do you think?" he asked, excited.

Removing her hands from his as he held the

opened journal, Aella said, "Let's check it out later, shall we?"

"You bet. I need you to do your psychic thing," he teased.

"Let me get coffee and breakfast from the café and we'll sit down and chart out some strategies, okay?"

Robert placed his hand on the small of her back. "Music to my ears. Let's go. I'll spring for a latte."

Laughing softly, Aella felt the warmth that exuded from this man. There was so much to appreciate about Robert. And his hand lightly grazing her back played hell with the love she felt for Fox. How was she going to deal with all of this?

Chapter 8

"There are limestone caves beneath the serpent mound. Did you know that?" Robert asked as he finished off his breakfast. Wiping his mouth with the paper napkin, he added, "My gut hunch is that if the emerald sphere is around here, it's in one of those caves."

Aella sipped her coffee. "Caves? Hey, now that is a possibility." She beamed at Robert, noticed how rugged he looked in his khaki long-sleeved shirt and trousers. There was something endearing about this man, Aella decided. When she contrasted her feelings toward Robert with those for Fox, there was no comparison. Fox had captured her whole heart. Her feelings for Fox were like nine billion glowing suns. When she looked a Robert, her heart responded to him like tepid tea. And before she'd known of her lifetime with Fox, Aella had felt much more drawn to Robert than she did now.

Sighing internally, she chewed on a piece of her cinnamon roll. "I could sit near the serpent and astrally travel into it. That way, I could check out the caves."

"I was hoping you could do something like that," he said, grinning.

"Being a shape-shifter, couldn't you?" she wondered.

"No, this is only a third-dimensional thing," he said. "I can change shape from man to cougar, but it's a physical change. I can't move into the other dimensions at will like you can."

"Still, that's a feat," she told him, pride in her tone. She watched him blush over her praise. Aella was sure that Robert had few people with whom he could share his mystical secret. In his profession, he'd be laughed at and humiliated. Some secrets needed to be kept.

"Well, it's a feat, but let's keep it in perspective," Robert chuckled. He spread open the map of the serpent before her. "Where do you want to start? We need a plan."

Pointing at the coiled tail, she said, "How about here? I'm good for about thirty minutes of astral travel and then I have to stop. By that time, I'm tired and I need to recharge. I can do another half hour the next morning. It will be slow this way, but I feel you're right: the sphere may be hiding in one of these caves."

"When Kendra got near to that old yew tree at Chalice Wells in Glastonbury," Robert pointed out, "the sphere unveiled itself. Her partner noted it was a full moon when it happened." He opened up a small almanac he pulled from another of his pockets. "According to this, we'll be getting a full moon in three days."

"Maybe we're right on time and didn't know

it," Aella murmured, sipping the last of her coffee. "Are you ready to get to work? What I need you to do is remain near me. If someone comes up and talks to me, it will jolt me out of my state. I'll slam back into my body and it's not a pleasant sensation. It will take me forty-eight hours to recover enough to try it again."

"I'll be your big, bad guard dog," he promised. Robert promised Aella he'd insure no human contact while she was in that state.

"Okay!" Aella said, scooping up the map, folding it and handing it back to him. "We've got a plan. Ready to get to work?" She was excited by the possibilities.

"You bet," he said, sliding out of the booth and standing up.

As they got out of their car, Aella relished the cool summer morning but her neck prickled with warning. Automatically she glanced around for any sign of danger.

"What?" Robert wondered, noting her furrowed brow. "Is something going on?"

"I don't know…" Aella sensed same dark, malevolent presence. "Something…someone…is watching us. It's a heavy energy, Robert."

"I don't feel anything," he said unhappily. "Shape-shifters have a lot of limitations."

Her mouth curved for a moment. "It's a male. I can feel his energy. He's watching us. And he wants something from us, but I don't know what."

Shutting the door, Robert walked to her side. "Don't worry about it. Probably just a local spirit, a discarnate who died around here and hasn't left to go to the Light yet. Come on, we need to get going."

Crossing the boundary into the park, Aella couldn't shake off the invisible intruder that seemed to follow them. She couldn't afford to expend any of her precious energy on trying to track the unseen and unwanted guest. On a given day, her aura produced only so much energy that could be utilized and she must save it today for the astral trip into the mound.

As they walked to the end of the snake, near the coil, Aella sensed Fox nearby. It would be impossible to talk with him further. She must focus on her task and not fritter away her energy on personal things. As much as she wanted to, Aella knew better. Finding her elm tree, Aella sat down on the towel Robert had spread out on the dewy grass. He was very thoughtful, and she nodded her thanks.

"Comfy?" he asked as he stood nearby. Above them, the end of the mound where the tail was coiled rose. The morning was fresh, the place quiet with only the sound of an inconstant breeze through the trees.

"Very," Aella said. "Stay about fifty feet away from me. Don't move around unless you have to. If someone comes toward us, go meet them and tell them I'm meditating and don't wish to be disturbed."

"Gotcha," Robert said. Aella was on the far side of the mound where few visitors ever came. Robert walked to the path at the tip of the mound and stood guard.

Satisfied, Aella closed her eyes, grounded herself and breathed deeply. The astral body fitted inside the human vessel. It took on the physical shape and expression in all ways. There were two ways the astral could leave. The first was through her solar-plexus chakra located in the region of her stomach. The better way was through the crown chakra located at the top of her head.

The feeling of the astral sliding out of her body was akin to someone pulling a glove from their hand. The body symbolized the glove and the hand was the astral form. The feeling of the astral easing up and out the top of her head was very real. Once it was free, she saw the silver cord that attached her astral to her physical form. The cord must remain connected between them. If it was cut or broken, she would instantly die. When a person died of natural causes, the silver cord disintegrated slowly over time, allowing the person's astral form to leave for the Light. Many people knew the Light as "heaven", depending upon their belief system.

The floaty feeling was wonderful and Aella always enjoyed astral travel. She could see into the fourth dimension now. Her heart sped up as she saw Fox standing nearby, a serious expression on his face; he seemed worried.

Good morning, Fox, she greeted as she hovered inches above the surface of the serpent mound. Her heart began to pound, crying out for him. There was an unexplicable connection between them and Aella didn't fight the feelings that surfaced for the mighty warrior.

Fox nodded. Just outside the periphery of the protective energy field around the mound stood Victor Guerra. He was in hunting mode and Fox could feel it. What was the sorcerer up to? He didn't know and it made him tense. From time to time, the sorcerer would pace the boundary, looking first at Robert and then at Aella. Shielding his worry, Fox said, *It is a good morning, Aella. How are you doing after our talk yesterday?* Fox saw and felt her heart energy surround him. The moment was intense, sweet, and flowed through him like a hot river of molten, glowing rock that

he'd once seen in the Andes. Her eyes widened and he could drown in their depths.
They made him want to love her slowly like
the clouds moving across the sky. Just to be
able to touch her, just once.... Fox stopped
his feelings. He loved Aella, his Chaska. An
ache moved through him like a thunderstorm
across the night-time jungle. Just to slide his
fingers across her jaw and feel her soft flesh.
To hold his lips close to her mouth and feel
the warmth of her breath upon him. Groaning
inwardly, Fox wrestled with his love.

I'm working my way through it, she signaled, mirth in her message to him. *Right now,
I'm going to astral-travel into the mound.
Robert says there are caves below it. He sus-
pects the emerald sphere might be hiding in
there. What do you think?*

Shrugging, Fox said, *It may be so. From
what you've told me about the sphere, it will
only show itself to the person who is supposed
to retrieve it, and, you must be very close for
it to trigger and respond. The caves below this*

*serpent are many. The people who built this
serpent here did so on purpose. The caves
represent the womb of Mother Earth and this
compounds the energy that is being sent constantly through this region. The caves amplify
the energy,* he explained.

*Ah, I see. Well, that does make sense. If
you'll excuse me, I must go to work now.*

Of course. Fox retreated. He went to the
boundary and faced Victor, who resembled a
jaguar on the prowl. The energy around the
sorcerer felt like a basket of heavy rocks.

*Get out of here, Guerra. You have no busi-
ness around here.*

Victor smirked at the warrior who stood inside the white, gauzy film of energy. *Indeed,
Guardian. Hide behind your shield. What I do
outside this place is none of your business.*

Fox held on to his mounting rage. In all
his years as the student in training, he'd never
seen the Dark Lord here. Now he's appeared
twice. *Why are you here? What interests you,
Guerra?*

Victor smiled, showing his long canine teeth. *That doesn't concern you, Guardian.*

Oh, it does. Very much so. These people are friends.

Snorting, Victor said, *You don't lie well, Guardian. I see you have eyes for that woman. She is much more than a friend.*

Holding onto his deteriorating patience, Fox knew there was only so much he could do. And Victor was much more powerful. It was an unbalanced situation protected only by the Light energy of the bubble surrounding the mound. Fox decided not to answer the grinning sorcerer. How much could Guerra see and know? The *Tupay* were barred from entry to the Akashic Records. Perhaps he was reading his aura? Possibly. Each had a shield up so they could not access the other's thoughts. Fox wasn't going to pass the time of day with this evil individual. Turning away, he made sure that his patrolling of the boundary area would continue so long as the *Tupay* was present.

* * *

"What did you find?" Robert asked excitedly as he sat down opposite Aella, who was feeling a bit groggy after returning to her body. Aella pushed some strands of hair away from her brow. "There's an incredible honeycomb of white limestone caves down there, Robert. In fact, I spent my time just walking around in the tail area. I didn't get far and I saw and felt nothing of the sphere."

"Can you draw what you saw?" He handed her the pencil and pad.

"Yes." Aella patiently sketched the scene for him. It usually took thirty minutes for her to feel back to normal after an astral journey. While the astral body needed to escape the heavy prison of the flesh in order to refresh and reenergize itself—usually with sleep—the reunion of spirit and flesh required adjustment.

The movement of the astral form was vital to the health of the physical body. When the astral body was out in the fourth dimension, it also brought the person dreams, visions and nightmares. A person with severe sleep deprivation hallucinated, but really saw into the fourth dimension. If the astral form failed to get the amount of time and renewable energy it needed to recharge, the physical vehicle suffered accordingly.

By contrast, when Aella took a conscious astral journey, her physical body was depleted of energy. The moment the astral body was out, it began to absorb, like a thirsty sponge, renewable energy. After she had slept six hours, she would feel invigorated and alert once more.

"This is fascinating," Robert said, excitement in his voice. He studied her simple drawing of the massive cave beneath the coiled tail. "Is this a dry or a wet cave?"

"Oh, it's wet," Aella said with a grin. "The limestone is still growing stalactites and stalagmites. I saw some beautiful forms in the tail and I also felt the energy running through this ley line times ten. It's really pulsating and pounding down there. The guardian told me before I went down there that the caves amplified the energy. He's right, it's a fierce, throbbing energy compared to that up here."

"Almost like a heart pumping blood," Robert murmured, studying the cave drawing. "We know Mother Earth has a heart and as it pumps deep within her core, she sends out pulsing beats of energy. That's what you felt, I'll bet."

Nodding, Aella got up and dusted off her jeans. It felt good to move around. Whenever her feather-light astral body came back into her human form, she felt incredibly heavy. Aella didn't like the sensation, but it couldn't be helped. The physical body was, after all, seen as a vehicle of sorts.

As she stood, she noticed a tall light of white and blue forming above the coil of the serpent. Frowning, she was shocked to realize that it was her chief guide, Athena, the goddess of wisdom. Turning, she looked down at Robert. "My guide is here. I need to go talk with her. I'll be right back."

"Sure," Robert said. He watched Aella walk

quickly toward the end of the serpent. Unable to see anything happening, he went back to studying her drawings of the cave structure.

I honor your presence, great goddess, Aella signaled as she saw the magnificent Greek goddess fully formed. Just as in the beautiful sculptures hewn by Greeks, Athena stood about fifteen feet tall. She wore a helmet of gold with a crest of blue horsehair in the center. Her gown glowed a bright white with intricate dark-blue embroidery across the front depicting the head of the Gorgon. At one side, she had a gold, oval shield with the Gorgon emblazoned upon it as well. Aella knew from past discussions with the goddess that the Gorgon, a woman whose head was filled with writhing snakes, was misrepresented by men. In reality the Gorgon symbolized the Great Mother Goddess. The hair of snakes symbolized her ability to create.

Later, patriarchal Greek scholars turned the Gorgon into something ugly and frightful. They wrote that if a man looked upon the head of the Gorgon, he would be frozen into eternity. Nothing could be further from the truth, for Aella knew that the Gorgon repented the Kundalini energy. This energy was given to all human beings and, like a coiled snake lying quietly in the base—or root chakra—of their spine, it could be awakened. When it was, the symbolic energy snake rose and wound through all the chakras of the human and up through their crown. Once this occurred, the person was connected in Oneness with the Mother Goddess. Enlightenment, compassion and spiritual evolution happened in an instant.

These people who had their Kundalini awakened became saints here on Earth. The halos around their heads were indicative of their sacred and divine connections with the Great Mother Goddess. The enlightened could heal others on all levels.

Bowing in reverence to the goddess, Aella asked, *What message do you bring me, Athena?*

Athena stared down at Aella. *Within the*

laws of the Great Mother I must warn you. Stay alert.

Aella understood that Athena could not give her specifics. To do so would be to stop her on her karmic path through this lifetime. She bowed to the goddess, who was resplendent with a glowing gold light infused with light blue. On Athena's left shoulder sat a barn owl. Her hand was wrapped around a gold spear. Even the owl watched her through its dark, starry, black eyes.

Thank you, Athena. I shall remain alert. I appreciate you being able to tell me this much. Go in peace, my goddess.

Athena smiled her approval as she faded from view. Within minutes, Aella was staring at the blue sky once more. She opened herself up to the energies at the mound. Earlier, she'd sensed danger. Now, her goddess had come to warn her as much as she could under the circumstances. What was out there beyond the serpent? Some evil entity was among them and Robert had jokingly passed it off as an unhappy

discarnate, a person who had lived, died, and
now refused to leave the earth plane.

Was it only a discarnate? Aella was no longer sure. Worriedly, she turned back as Robert
was getting up. She tried to see Fox, but could
not. It was just as well since she was exhausted
and needed to go back to rest at the motel.
The nagging fear in her gut wouldn't go away.
The alarm within her grew stronger. Now, for
the first time Aella was really scared.

"Robert, there's a problem," she told him
as he walked up to her. Rapidly, she shared
Athena's warning.

Robert glanced around. "Funny, I don't feel
any sense of danger. The robins are singing,
the day is beautiful. I don't question what you
got, I just can't sense it. Sorry."

"That's okay," Aella said, reaching out and
squeezing his upper arm. She saw his eyes go
dark with longing—for her. Yes, she was un-
questionably drawn to Robert. But now, the
memory of her ancient deep love for Fox colored everything, for better or worse.

"Let's go back to the motel. You need to rest," he told her, giving her a worried look. "You're pale."

Aella fell into step at his side. "I'm spent. A lot is going on and I can't sort it all. I wish I could, but my psychic batteries are fried for a while. I'm basically off line for six hours, Robert." And with her goddess showing up to warn her of something dire, Aella felt helpless. Until she got her rest, all she had were the hairs standing up on the back of her neck to warn her that something evil was lurking nearby.

Fox wanted to scream, but he couldn't. It was impossible to reach Aella because of the work she'd done in the caves. He followed the couple trying desperately to get their attention. In the parking lot, near their car, Victor Guerra hovered like a vulture waiting to attack. And Fox knew he would. Once he left the protection of the energy around the mound, Fox was just as vulnerable as the two humans. He simply did not have the kind of celestial power Victor had swirling around him. Victor had thousands of sorcerers on Earth and in the fourth dimension who fueled him with huge loads of expendable energy.

As he watched them walk out of the protective bubble, Fox's heart turned in his chest. Aella was in danger! There was nothing he could do to protect her! A scream clawed up into Fox's throat as he hovered inches above the sidewalk, still protected by the Light energy.

Aella and Robert walked across the asphalt parking lot, oblivious to the fact that Guerra would do something terrible in the next few minutes. Frantic, Fox paced the boundary. He saw the look of glee on Guerra's narrow face. The pointed goatee only accentuated the sorcerer's triangular, dark-brown face. It was his smile, more of a grimace, the long canines showing, that made Fox shiver in dread. He had no idea what the sorcerer was planning. As the Dark Lord, Guerra could kill both of them.

Tears of terror jammed into Fox's eyes. If

he tried to stop the sorcerer, Guerra would kill him just as easily. And then the mound would be left without a guardian. The pumping of energy around Mother Earth's etheric was prime. Fox could not walk away from his responsibility. It would leave the sacred site open to the *Tupay* if he left. And he couldn't do that—not even for the woman he loved with every breath.

"Here we are," Robert said, opening the door for Aella. "It's almost lunchtime. Let's go to the motel, you take a nap, recover and when you wake up, I'll buy you dinner. How about that?" he teased, smiling down at her.

Aella tried to smile, but it was impossible. How to communicate to Robert this overwhelming sense of terror over an attack that she knew was coming? As she opened her mouth to speak, a dark cloud appeared out of the blue sky just above them. A strangled sound clawed up her throat. Eyes bulging, she saw the shape become a man in black clothing. The look in his dead black eyes frightened her more than anything else. This was Victor Guerra, the Dark Lord. She knew it was him from the depths of her soul.

"Robert!" she screamed, pointing upward, "look out!"

Chapter 9

Robert felt a sudden, stunning blow to the top of his head. He uttered a gasp, staggered back and collapsed onto the asphalt like a rag doll. The energy pummeling through him was something he'd never experienced in his life. His vision dimmed. Struggling, he felt himself expanded inside, like a balloon being blown up. All his organs groaned and were squished and pinned against the inner wall of his body. His skin stretched and he wondered if it would tear open. What was going on?

He heard Aella's cry. Panicked, Robert could tell something terrible was happening to him. The word *attack* slammed through him. How could he stop this sensation? Knowing it was an invasion by some entity, he fought blindly to stop it. He could not.

Aella shrieked as she watched Robert fall. He lay on the asphalt, his face drained of its usual dark suntan. She felt an evil presence. Frantic, she looked around. Was Robert dead? What was happening to him? His limbs twitched violently, as if he were having a seizure. Kneeling over him, she shook his shoulders.

"Robert! Robert! Wake up! Wake up! Tell me what's going on."

Her voice cracked, and she sat back on her heels as his eyes suddenly opened. They look turgid and murky. Weakly, he raised his arm and then it flopped back down on the asphalt.

"Where…" he croaked, trying to look around.

Touching his sweaty brow, Aella whispered,

"Robert? Are you all right? What happened? Are you hurt?"

He slowly sat up, groaning, his hands against his head. "I—"

It was as if he had been wrestling internally with something. What had happened? The feeling of evil had disappeared. Her own sixth sense was dulled by overwork. She couldn't do anything right now except rest and recharge. Again, Aella tried to fathom what had happened to Robert. Frustrated that her powers were at low ebb, she watched as Robert sat up groggily, his head resting on his drawn-up knees. Aella stood and rested a protective hand against his shoulder.

"Can you tell me what happened, Robert?"

Victor laughed to himself. He violently suppressed Robert's spirit—it was much stronger than he'd anticipated. Situating himself into the man's body, Victor enjoyed the strength of this masculine specimen. And he liked the pleasurable touch of Aella's hand on his shoulder. Looking through the man's eyes, Victor reoriented himself to being back into a human form once more. It always felt like a heavy weight cloaked around his spirit. He hated that sensation, but as his feather-light spirit adjusted to the physical vehicle, it would feel less dense and would become easier to endure.

Victor used more of his power to keep Robert's spirit silent. *He* spoke instead to Aella.

"I'm okay, Aella. I just had a moment of dizziness. Give me a few more minutes, and I'll be fine."

Unsure, Aella did indeed see Robert's features returning to their normal color. "Can I get you anything?"

Robert looked up and gave her a weak smile. "Just your presence is enough."

The rejoinder struck Aella as odd. Maybe the fall or the dizziness had addled Robert. "Do you want me to take you to the nearest emergency room? Just to be checked over?"

Raising his hand, Robert said, "No, no. Don't bother." Victor laughed. "Listen, in Egypt when

I was at a dig in the middle of summer, I had sunstroke. I survived it. So, don't worry, okay? I get dizzy spells every once in a while. It's nothing. I'm sorry I didn't tell you about them before."

Aella went over and picked up his hat. "You're sure?" She handed the hat to him, and he placed it on his head.

"Positive." Looking around, Victor saw Robert's guardian, the cougar, ready to attack him. Well, it was too little, too late. No chief guide could stop the Dark Lord himself from taking over a body it was charged with protecting. Chief guides were powerful but certainly not nearly as powerful as he was. The cougar leaped at him, her paws outstretched, claws coming at him. Lifting his finger, he sent a powerful beam of energy at the cat. In an instant, it exploded into light and sparks. Gone. Victor lowered his arm and smiled to himself. That spirit cat was now back at the Village of the Clouds. It would have to rest for a period after being zapped by him. And then it would be assigned to someone else.

As Victor sat in Robert's body, he felt the man's struggling spirit. Victor used more of his energy to squash the spirit into imprisoned passivity. He oriented to Aella who stood near him, seeming anxious. What a fine specimen of woman she was. He could feels his loins tightening. My! He had missed being in a man's body for some time now. Ever since he'd lost his own body down in Peru in a battle with his daughter, Ana, he'd remained in spirit. Oh, he'd possessed other human bodies now and then when necessary, but only for an hour or a few days. When he left the body, it died within five minutes. And when he got through with Robert's body, the same thing would happen to him.

"Would you like some water?" Aella asked, still frightened for her partner even though he seemed better. His eyes cleared and he appeared to be present once again. Had it been a dizzy spell caused by sunstroke? Aella wasn't a medical person so she really didn't know.

Robert got to his feet, gave her a sheepish look and dusted off the back of his khaki pants. "No, I'm fine. Really." He reached out and grazed her cheek with his fingertips. "Thanks for caring. That was very sweet of you, Aella."

Aella's cheek tingled beneath his unexpected touch. Something was different about Robert, but she couldn't understand what. His eyes were narrowed upon her. Aella swore she felt a wave of lust coming from him. It deluged her and she felt disgusted by it.

"Let's get you back to the motel," she said abruptly. "I'll drive."

Victor cursed inwardly. He'd moved too fast on Aella. Oh, he wanted this beauty in his bed, and he wanted to be inside her hot, tight confines. And he'd get her there sooner or later. "Of course. Let's go," he said, opening the passenger-side door. What Victor wanted even more was for Aella was to locate the emerald sphere.

Aella parked the car at the motel. Shaken and not knowing why, she turned to Robert. "Will you be all right?"

"Of course," he said, smiling. "I'm going to go lie down." He glanced at his watch. "How about we go rest, and then we'll meet at six for dinner?"

"That's fine," she said.

"I'll look forward to later," he said, flashing his most charming smile.

Helplessness sliced through Fox like a knife gutting his abdomen. Standing at the periphery of the protective light energy around the mound, he'd seen the attack by Victor Guerra upon the man. Robert didn't stand a chance against the violent power of the Dark Lord. And there had been nothing Fox could do. He knew that the sorcerer was taking a chance by possessing the archeologist. If Robert's karma had not left this path of possibility open, then Victor would have been stopped from entering him.

That didn't stop Fox from trying to alert

Aella. When he saw her aura, especially around her head, he realized her exhaustion. Even as he valiantly tried to alert her, her fatigue would hinder her efforts to perceive the attack by Victor.

Victor threw up an energy shield around Aella, which blocked Fox's telepathic warning. With a hiss, Fox tried again and again. Each time, the master sorcerer sent his warning back to him. Nothing could reach Aella right now and Fox understood that only too well. His training as a jaguar warrior had enabled him to build a mental toughness that allowed him to send or receive messages from the emperor no matter how mentally exhausted he was. But Aella did not have that training. No, when she used up her psychic skills, they would need time to replenish. By then Victor would be so well hidden within Robert that she would never be able to know he'd been possessed. Worse, Fox knew that Victor would throw up that shield to stop Fox's warning from reaching her.

Feeling helpless, Fox walked back toward

the mound. Robert's spirit had wanted this possession experience for whatever unknown reason. Once Guerra fled the man's body, he would die in five minutes. The silver cord would automatically be cut by the sorcerer as he left the human vehicle. Fox could do nothing to help.

Sighing, he walked to his hut but didn't want to go inside just yet. Fox sat down on a crudely hewn stool he'd carved many years earlier. The day was sunny. The rays slanted through the overhead woodland that surrounded the sacred site. He could hear the birds singing and saw them flitting through the trees. Many of the bird babies had fledged and were learning to find their own meals. There was such peace and harmony, but his mind spun with dread. If Robert could be possessed, what plans did Victor have for Aella?

That thought devastated Fox as nothing else ever would. It was unimaginable that he should lose his wife once again. As he sat there, he felt a new energy entering the mound. Sitting up, he frowned. A golden light appeared in front of him. Eventually, it took the shape of Grandmother Alaria. Hope flared inside Fox. He stood, bowed and thought, *Grandmother, it is good to see you after what has just happened.*

Alaria wore her usual blue robe that fell to her sandaled feet. Her last lifetime had been as a Druid priestess on the Isle of Mona near Great Britain. When the Romans had sacked the sacred island where all knowledge of Druidism was kept, she had been killed trying to save the many scrolls from the fires set by the soldiers. Her silver hair fell in two braids across her thin shoulders. She wore a white alpaca cloak.

Alaria and her husband, Adaire, had been the chief Druids at Mona. Adaire had died as well. Their spirits were taken by the Great Mother Goddess to the Village of the Clouds where they were interned as leaders of the mystical place of Light. There, they had continued the metaphysical schooling of spirits as well as of humans who visited, either in person or astrally during their sleep cycle.

My son, I felt your fear, Alaria telepathed. She smiled and walked up to Fox. *As you can see, there is a greater plan unfolding here at the place you protect.*

Yes, Grandmother, I see it and I'm worried for Aella....

Alaria held up her hand. *Fox, you must stand aside. This is your final test to see if you can truly become the trusted guardian of a sacred site. This test asks you to not interfere. I know how much you love Chaska. I have searched the Akashic Records and you must know that her path has options that she may take in this life. And there is* nothing *you can do about this, my son.* She drilled him with a knowing look. *You do understand what that means, Fox? The Dark Lord was allowed entrance into Robert. The archeologist has a spiritual path to follow and choices to make as well. You must remain inside the protection*

*of Light around this sacred mound. There is
no way you can interfere. If you do, you will
have failed the test and will set karma in mo-
tion for all of us.*

Fox paced back and forth in front of his
hut. *Frankly, Grandmother, having to sit and
watch Aella be stalked by the Dark Lord himself is just too much of a test! No one can expect me to stand by and just watch her be hurt
or killed by Guerra!*

*That is exactly what you must do, Fox.
Stand by. Do NOT interfere.*

Angrily, Fox turned on the elder. *What is so
much more important than the love I hold for
Chaska? Nothing!* As he cut his hand through
the air as if he were carrying a sword, Fox's
breath came in short bursts of anger and frustration.

*If you do not pass this test, you know what
will happen.*

Fox gave her a twisted smile. *So what if
I de-evolve back into human form? I don't*

find that as much of a sentence as you might, Grandmother.

Nodding, Alaria gave him a sympathetic look as she folded her hands in front of her. *My son, each of us are tested in some unique way known only to our soul. I was tested. So was Adaire. We all are. And the test, when it comes, is horrific. If you fail this test, you will go back into endless incarnation cycles once more on Earth. And you will stay on that path until your soul decides to try again to rise above the flesh of human existence. Is that what you really want? You've earned the right to be here. Please, my son, do not fail this test.*

I don't find loving someone a failure, Fox said bitterly. *And perhaps my soul does not yet understand that it can stand by helplessly and watch the one I love violated and killed.*

Alaria sighed. *I understand your dilemma, Fox. We all create the ultimate test by wanting to go back instead of moving forward spiritually. The test is seen as too hard, too brutal and truly will rip our heart apart. Somehow,*

*you must find strength and faith to pull your-
self through this awful time of testing.*

Fox stopped his pacing. He dearly loved
Grandmother Alaria. She was the soul of
warmth, much like the sun upon his body.
He saw the compassion in her blue eyes and
in the soft set of her lips. He understood she
needed to remind him of the path he'd chosen. Lowering his voice, he opened his hands
and said, *Grandmother, I cannot stand by and
watch Chaska hurt by the Dark Lord. I simply
cannot.*

*Wait and see what transpires, my son. Have
faith in the unknown. You have up until now.
Allow the honesty of all the players to be revealed before you make a choice.*

Simple, honest words, Fox thought. His
mouth tasted of ashes. Of terror for Aella. In
his gut, he knew the Dark Lord would harm
or kill her. He gave Grandmother Alaria a
kind look. *Perhaps I made the wrong choice.
I have been looking at what I've done and I'm
not happy. I was happy as a jaguar warrior.*

I liked my Earth lives. I know I suffered in many of them, but ultimately, I was happy. I'm not happy here, Grandmother. Fox gestured around the sacred site. *I'm bored here. I'm restless. There is not much to do even with Chima away for further schooling at your village.*

I see...well, I pray that you do the right thing, Fox.

Fox bowed to the elder. *Thank you for coming, Grandmother. I know your help is needed in so many other more important places than mine.*

Alaria's expression was filled with love. Alaria said, *Oh, my son, you are equally important. Always. Don't ever forget that you are greatly loved. These tests are hard on the soul. I pray you transcend the doubt, your boredom and the desire to step into Aella's karmic path. Try to have hope and faith in the greater plans of our Mother.*

Fox watched Alaria's form begin to dissolve into a cloud of white and gold light. It faded from view, leaving him with the sun shining brightly overhead in the blue July sky. Shaking his head, he went into his hut to lie down for a while. He needed time to sort all this out. Worst of all, his heart ached for Aella. She was in great danger and probably didn't even know what had happened. Would she realize Guerra had possessed Robert? Fox understood a human had only so much psychic energy and couldn't always perceive things correctly or in time. Lying down on his pallet, he rested his arm across his eyes and felt like crying.

"Maybe your next astral journey should be at the head of the snake," Robert said. "What do you think?" He ate his steak and potato dinner voraciously as they sat in the local restaurant. It was nearly empty of patrons, the noise level tolerable. In the hours alone with Robert's spirit, Victor had had to use even more of his energy to keep the archeologist's spirit controlled. The extra effort angered him until he looked over at Aella, who seemed refreshed from her nap. All this struggle was worth it. "The snake has its mouth open and there is an egg that it is going to swallow," he added.

Aella agreed with him and picked at her shrimp salad. She wasn't really hungry. The rest had given her renewed energy, although she knew she wasn't in tiptop shape yet. She needed a full night's sleep to get there. "If that is so, what about if I journey into the egg itself, Robert? The possibility of the emerald sphere being in the egg is more intriguing to me."

"Hmm, you may be right," Robert said, adding sour cream and butter to his baked potato. It was obvious to him that Aella was like a cosmic bird dog, able to scent out the emerald sphere. Eventually, she would lead him to the right place. "All right, how about tomorrow morning we go to the egg part of the mound? I'll stand guard and you do your thing—check and see if there is a cave under the egg?"

Sipping her lemon iced tea, Aella nodded. Robert seemed fine. She still felt a mix of confusing energy around him. She could see some of his aura, but not all of it, simply because her energy level was too low. His aura, generally quite sunny with clean colors in the astral field, looked like stirred-up mud. When a person was ill, his aura became murky, but Robert appeared quite robust and filled with incredible energy.

"When you've had these dizzy episodes in the past did you always feel ten times better afterward?" she wondered aloud.

Robert grinned. "Yes. Isn't that something? It can fell me like an ox, but give me an hour and look at me." He flexed his arms and felt the muscles responding. That sent a frisson of pride through Victor. Indeed, this was a very nice masculine vehicle he'd chosen to possess.

Aella watched his biceps bulge and smiled. Such a likeable man. It would be so much easier to fall in love with him. "Yes, you've certainly recovered. There's no doubt about that."

Victor shared her grin and resumed eating his dinner. As much as he wanted to haul her into his bed, have her soft, curvy body beneath his, all that would have to wait. The pain in his loins was very real and Victor silently salivated as he looked deep into her golden eyes. Truly, even though she was a Warrior for the Light, he would find great joy in turning her to the Dark. Warriors who made love with *Tupay,* lost their status and became *Tupay* themselves. It would be a delightful turn, for Victor could use someone of Aella's considerable talents....

Aella moaned and tossed in bed that night. Fox came to her in a dream. He would make sure she would not recall it after she awoke.

Beloved, I want to share when we met for the first time. Allow me to show you that....

The mist in front of Aella changed. Once more she saw herself as spirited Chaska, only this time, she was fourteen years old. Under her arm, she was carrying fruit from near the Lunar Temple down at the Urubambu River.

Turning, she saw the boy, now a strong young man, ease out from behind the stone temple.

With a gasp, Chaska dropped the basket. There was talk of jaguars who lived near the temple by the river. Aella had ignored her mother's warnings to pick ripe fruit along the banks of the river.

"Wait! Do not be afraid of me, Chaska."

The boy held up his hand. He quietly padded on bare feet toward her. "My name is Atok Sopa. I saw you many years ago. Remember? When you ran down toward the jaguar warrior's cave?"

Gulping, Chaska bent down and nervously started picking up the papayas and putting them back into her basket. "Yes, I do." Her eyes rounded as she looked up at him. Atok was a strapping young warrior. He had a toughness in his chocolate eyes and the way his mouth was set. Like all initiates into the mysteries of the jaguar cult, Atok wore a leather thong with a gold jaguar's head on his broad chest. A black cotton skirt fell from his waist to just above his knees. Indeed, Chaska thought him to be incredibly beautiful in a man's way.

Leaning down, Atok picked up the rest of the yellowish fruit and put them in the basket. He remained crouched, only a foot's distance separating them. "You are so beautiful. I found out your name and I say a prayer for you every morning, Chaska."

Touched, Chaska felt heat racing into her cheeks. Automatically, she touched one of them. "I—I shouldn't be talking with you. We could get into trouble."

He gave her a wicked smile and slowly looked around. "Trust me, no one knows I am here. I know how to be invisible. Even my master teacher cannot find me."

"How did you find me?" she gasped.

Reaching out his fingers, he lightly touched her flaming cheek. He could feel the heat of her skin. "Because we are connected through time to one another, my beloved Chaska. You feel it, don't you? I know you do."

Just the skimming touch of his caress across her cheek made her heart race furiously in her chest. Chaska had never been touched like this. Indeed, in her royal family she was a virgin and would remain such until she was given away in marriage to some powerful lord in the empire. "I—uh—I feel that my heart will leap out of my chest," she admitted breathlessly. Drowning in the chocolate pools of his eyes, Chaska felt that connection. It was grounding. Startling. Beautiful. Exciting.

"Yes," Atok whispered, suddenly choked up with emotion. He reluctantly withdrew his hand from her cheek. "Sweet, wonderful Chaska, you are mine. I will send you dreams, my beloved. Dreams of you and I. Hold on to them. They are my heart on wings of a condor to your spirit…."

Chapter 10

Fox watched apprehensively from the boundary of the mound. Aella and Robert, who now had Victor possessing his every move, climbed out of their car. As he read her aura, he gauged that Aella was all right. Had Victor really left her alone? As much as he wanted to, Fox was forbidden from leaving. He would lose his job and face severe punishment. Humiliation would be heaped upon his head by his peers. Still, Fox had considered breaking the rules, such was his love for Chaska.

As the night on Earth had worn on, Fox had asked himself serious questions. Was there a boundary on love? Could any law, even a cosmic one set by the Great Mother herself, override love? When could a soul turn away from love in the name of duty and responsibility? Fox didn't know and he was confused. He had no one to speak to about this quandary. No one to give him answers, but he understood that this was the ultimate test before he locked into his new spiritual level of growth. He must search within himself, find the answers and make the correct choices.

Relief flooded him as he looked again at Aella's aura. For now, she was safe. Victor would be allowed into the sacred site precisely because he was in a human form. That law should be changed. As he noted the lurid red-brown color in Robert's aura, Fox felt deep compassion for the spirit of the man.

Stepping back, Fox felt it important to confront Victor. As Robert and Aella walked into the mound area, penetrating the protective bubble, Fox rushed at Robert.

Halting, Victor saw the jaguar warrior's savage features. His eyes burned with a hatred that Victor was used to meeting on the field of battle with warriors for the Light. *Begone, Guardian. I'm here legitimately and there's nothing you can do about it.* Victor laughed.

Hatred welled up in Fox. Standing above Robert, he hissed, *The moment you make a mistake, Guerra, I will be here to take advantage of it.*

I won't make any mistakes. In fact, you should know that as soon as Aella finds the emerald sphere, it is mine. He laughed derisively.

Aella glanced at Robert. She sensed he was in communication with someone. There was a gleam in his eyes she'd never seen before. Uncomfortable, she asked, "Robert? Is everything all right?"

Robert seemed distracted. "What? Oh, yes, everything's fine."

"You're telepathically talking to someone? Your chief guide?"

Robert smiled. "Yes, I was," he lied. Victor didn't want to tell the delicate Aella that the cougar was no more, that the great cat's spirit was now part of the cycle of Light, to be reborn and serve another human. He took her elbow and pointed toward the mouth of the serpent to their right. "Come on, let's get to work. Aren't you excited about this?"

She pulled her elbow out of Robert's hand. All morning, he'd found reasons to touch her lightly on the cheek, the shoulder, the small of her back. Although she wanted his touches, she wanted to initiate them, on her terms. He just seemed different and that confused her. "Yes, I'm looking forward to exploring beneath the egg this morning."

"And you got a good night's sleep?"

"Very good. Deep." Aella wanted to say, no dreams from Fox. And perhaps that was just as well. She had sensed Fox's nearness but had not used her psychic ability to perceive him.

She had to keep her energy contained for the thirty-minute astral travel session in order to search the cave, if there was one, beneath the egg in the jaws of the serpent's open mouth.

They walked around to the front of the five-foot-high grassy mound. At 8:00 a.m. there were no other visitors nor would there likely be until an hour from now. She heard the trilling of a robin in a nearby buckeye tree. In the egg a redbud tree grew. It was small and spindly, but then, that type of tree didn't get very big. In the spring, the redbud tree would have tiny pink flowers covering it long before the heart-shaped leaves appeared. Now, at fifteen feet tall and with a reddish-brown trunk, it looked like any other Ohio tree from the surrounding woodlands.

"Robert? Don't the Native Americans who live in this region consider the redbud tree sacred?"

"Yes, yes they do," Victor said, pulling that information from Robert's spirit. The lovely thing about possession was that Victor had all the knowledge accrued by that spirit. He could delve into Robert's imprisoned spirit and steal information when he needed it.

"Many other nations consider the cotton-wood tree sacred," he told her amiably as she sat down under an elm tree about fifty feet in front of the egg. "Up here," he said, gesturing around the area, "the redbud tree holds the same sacredness for these nations."

Pressing her back against the trunk, Aella smiled up at Robert. He had his usual note-book in hand, the pens in his left pocket. "It's a beautiful tree. Small but pretty. Okay, I'm ready to astral travel."

Dipping his head, Robert said, "Good. I'll keep everyone away from you so it doesn't distract your investigation."

Aella watched Robert walk away. He headed toward the gate where people would eventually come in after paying their entrance fee. The entire area was ringed with a fence and all people were funneled into this one area. It was a good tactical move on his part; he could ensure no one would wander over and bother her.

Sighing, Aella closed her eyes, grounded herself and started the process. One part of her, that silly, romantic heart of hers, wanted to take time to find Fox and talk with him. To do that, of course, would be selfish. Even if they had been entwined lovers, two parts of the same soul coming together to love one another eternally, nothing could be done about it. She'd lain awake last night chewing over the dilemma.

She ached to see and hear Fox once more, but how would that help? She'd spent most of yesterday trying to reconcile the anguish, the grief and loss of him. This morning she'd awakened to realize that the past was exactly that. Didn't do a bit of good to pine.

As she inhaled deeply to move into the altered state of consciousness, Aella concentrated on her task.

There was a soft "pop" as she exited her physical body through the top of her head.

Aella headed down through the large egg. Because she was in the fourth dimension now, she could move through dirt and rock as if it weren't there.

As she drifted downward, she spotted a cave. It was dark, but in this dimension, she could see clearly as if sunlight were filling the limestone chamber. Standing just above the yellow and white limestone floor, she looked around. The drip, drip, drip of the water caught her attention. Stalactites hung like sharpened spears around the oval cave. The floor was nubby with spikes, large and small, created from the water constantly dripping from the roof.

Aella felt the coolness. The astral body was her emotional vehicle and her six senses would register. Aella was moved by the beauty of the cavern. How had the natives of this region known about it? At one time, had these caves been open and viewable? They must have been.

As she slowly walked around, Aella noticed

a rectangular altar at the very end of the cave. She could see through the dirt and rock and view the egg built above the cave.

The altar was made of yellow and white limestone rocks. It was about four feet high and four feet in rectangular width. Each stone had been lovingly shaped and honed into a rectangle with a symbol inscribed. One had a wolf, another a cougar, a vulture, a robin. Though she admired the skilled handiwork, Aella was puzzled that she found nothing on top of the altar.

This cave had to have an opening to the outside world. Otherwise, how could this altar have been built? On the floor, she perused the nubby area around the altar. A number of sharpened points had long ago been broken off by someone walking over them. Over time, drips of water from the ceiling had re-established those pointed stalagmites.

Aella drifted just above the floor of the cave and walked around the altar. What had it been used for? She couldn't tell how it was important. Was this where the emerald sphere was located? She tried to sense it, but nothing indicated it was here. Frustrated, Aella walked beyond the altar to a corridor between the egg-cave chamber and another one beneath the head of the serpent.

She could feel herself tiring. How quickly thirty minutes flew by! As she left the cave, Aella moved gently back into her physical body, feet first through the crown of her head. She made sure her astral form went at a pace that would not send any shocks reverberating through her. As her astral feet locked into her human feet, she opened her eyes and allowed the heaviness to settle within her body. It would take about five minutes more for her to orient back to the here and now of the third dimension.

A robin was singing nearby. The sweet smell of dewy grass, the sun rising in the July sky, all served to reorient her. She pressed her hands into the grass feeling its long, soft, damp texture. Looking to her right, she saw Robert walking in her direction, his expression keen and interested.

"Well?" he urged, kneeling down in front of her, "How did it go? Did you find it?" Victor wanted that sphere. He searched her drowsy features. It was tough for any human to consciously astral travel. He had to curb his interest because her eyes were still dull from the journey.

Aella sat up and reached for the bottle of water in her knapsack. "I didn't see anything except a rock altar." She found herself tremendously thirsty and drank.

"An altar?" Robert asked. "Was there anything on it?"

Shaking her head, Aella reported what she had seen. He seemed disappointed and she felt that way, too. "Your idea of going to the egg was very smart. I thought for sure the sphere would be there."

Robert sat down. "But the altar's in there. They were using it for something."

"At one time, yes," Aella agreed. She

watched long, white high clouds beginning to drift across the blue sky, muting the sunlight a bit. Already she could feel the humidity of the summer morning climbing.

Taking off his hat, Robert scratched his head in thought. "Okay, an altar is a good indicator there was a ceremony taking place down there in the past. Yet, you saw nothing else around it?"

"No, the place was clean. There was no debris, no nothing."

"Damn." He noticed Aella's disappointment. Realizing too late that Robert did not curse, he added, "Sorry…"

"You're just disappointed," Aella said. "So am I."

Curbing his frustration, Victor watched the guardian hover nearby. The energy around the jaguar warrior was intense and filled with hatred. Victor smiled briefly—there was nothing he could do. A sense of deep satisfaction flowed through him and he savored the guardian's helplessness. "Could you do this again?"

he pressed. "I feel that if the sphere isn't in the egg, then it must be in the head of this serpent." Anxiously, he sent her a tremendous wave of energy meant to sway her to what he wanted.

Aella felt instantly uncomfortable. This was a different energy, heavy and filled with desire to get her to say yes. Aella had never experienced something like this before. "No, I can't possibly do that, Robert. You know that." Her irritation surfaced. He should have known better.

Victor held up his hands in apology. "I'm sorry. Of course, you're right. We need to get you back to the motel to rest." He stood and held out his hand to her. "Come on, enough's been done for today." So, this woman was not really as powerful as Victor had assumed. She had a very short psychic time span in which to work and that buoyed him. Victor had thought the foundation would send very powerful people on a mission like this. In the end, Aella was weak in comparison to a true sorcerer.

Joy thrummed through him. This made his job easier. Robert was certainly weak.

In many ways, Victor could let his guard down. The one with the real power, however, was that site guardian. Victor knew that, as a previous jaguar warrior, he was nearly equal to himself. Cosmic laws being what they were, though, even the guardian had limits to where he could use his power. Snickering to himself, Victor mentally rubbed his hands with delight. This time, he could taste the victory. This time, he would get the emerald sphere. There was no one to stop him.

Fox felt relief as Victor left the protection zone around the mound. He hated the fact the sorcerer's hand was on Aella's elbow guiding her back to their car. Fox's skin crawled, and he felt sick inside. Victor could easily kill her, too, and the sorcerer was waiting for her to find the emerald sphere. He wished, for the thousandth time, that he knew where it was. Even old Chima knew nothing because Fox had telepathed the question to him. Chima had told him that the Emerald Key necklace spheres would never divulge themselves to anyone of the Light or Dark—only to the one person who was supposed to retrieve each emerald. Until then, Fox could feverishly hunt up and down the mound, but he would never locate them.

Frustration thrummed through Fox. He weighed alternatives, none of them good. He loved Aella so much that it consumed him. There were no thoughts other than protecting her spirit. Fox would gladly give his spirit's life for hers. There was no question Victor would do anything to get that sphere from Aella. And if Fox had to give his life, he would, to protect her.

Despite all this, Fox knew that a spirit could never really be killed. Energy could never be destroyed, only changed in mass and quality. It was a huge sacrifice to give one's spiritual life for another. And Fox had seen it happen before. Grandmother Alaria had told him that someone from the Village of the Clouds had rescued the fallen Light spirit and taken it back to the village. Many hours of intense healing work was undertaken in order to bring back the energy of that spirit. Of course, once the spirit gave its energetic life for something, it could never go back. There was a rehabilitation period for the recobbled spirit. After becoming whole again, with the help of the soul, the spirit was then put back into service, and would choose to learn another skill in order to continue its advancement toward Oneness with the Great Mother Goddess.

His heart burst with such love for Aella that Fox decided to break a law. Somehow, he had to warn her of Victor and his diabolical intentions!

Aella quickly fell asleep. She was tired from the day's activities. Robert seemed aggressively concerned about the search for the sphere. Much more so than in earlier days. He'd worn on her sensitivity and she was much more tired than usual.

Her dream started almost immediately. She saw a replay of her and Robert from the other day in the parking lot. Only this time, a man in dark clothes hovered above them, his black eyes dead as he watched them like a wolf salivating over a quarry. The feeling around this man frightened her. Aella saw his aura fully and that scared her even more. The word, *sorcerer* kept repeating itself in her dream.

As she looked at the dark-clothed man, his narrow face brown, his goatee accentuating the shape of his head, Aella wanted to scream. He watched Robert intently. He lunged downward and Aella gasped. She witnessed the sorcerer hitting Robert, going through his crown chakra and possessing his body. Robert fell to the pavement. Only this time, Aella saw the terrible battle that ensued in those few moments afterward. Robert's spirit fought mightily against the savage intruder. And then, to her horror, the sorcerer killed Robert's cougar guardian. The spirit exploded into gold and white light and then disappeared.

Heart beating hard in her breast, Aella rose. Gasping, her hand against her silky nightgown over her heart, she looked around. Fear ate at her. Perspiration dotted her wrinkled brow. Shakily, Aella threw off the sheet, the breeze from the air conditioner cooling her skin. Great Goddess, what had just happened? Was this dream real? A figment of her imagination? Aella wasn't sure. She turned on the lamp at the bedside and padded to the bathroom.

As she looked into the mirror, she noted the dark circles beneath her eyes. Feeling as if she were being stalked even now, she quickly twisted the handles of the faucet. She splashed tepid water across her face and dried off before trying to reorient. Okay, it was a dream. But was it real? Was it her imagination? Sometimes, Aella couldn't tell. Had Fox sent it to her? Was this Fox's jealousy or a warning?

Unsure, Aella hung the towel on the rack and shut off the light. As she stood in the middle of the room, she tried to understand the dream. At least she could read it symbolically.

Many dreams were about the subconscious talking to the conscious being in the language of symbols. Ever since Robert had fallen after being dizzy, he had been different. Had her subconscious created this dream to explain why? That would make sense, Aella thought as she sat down on the edge of the bed.

What if the dream were literal? What if Robert had been possessed? Aella remembered the mission briefing and how Victor Guerra had possessed Kendra once she had the sphere. Or, was this her overactive imagination taking that event and putting a twist on it? Maybe just the threat of it happening had inspired the dream.

That had to be it.

Feeling better, Aella turned off the lamp, eased back into bed and pulled the sheet up and over her shoulders once more. She snuggled down into the pillow, confident that the building pressure and stress was the reason for the upsetting dream. After all, she knew Guerra might appear, but it was impossible for him to broach a sacred place. Sighing softly, she turned on her right side and closed her eyes. Aella was convinced the dream was a pressure-release valve and not really the threat she thought it was.

Chaska!

Chaska turned at the low growl of a man's voice behind her. At seventeen, she had grown taller than most of the women at the temple. She had gone down to the Lunar Temple at the river to send her prayers for her grandmother who lay dying at their stone house. She was forty-five years old and riddled with arthritis. Tears flowed down Chaska's cheeks as she heard her name called.

Her eyes widened. There, hidden in the jungle, was Atok Sopa! Gasping, she got off her knees, her woolen robe falling to her ankles. "Atok!" It had been a year since she'd last seen him. He'd tried to steal moments away from his intense and deadly training to talk with her. She saw him give her a confident smile and leap out of the dark, vine-ridden jungle. How handsome he was! This year he was to graduate and become a proud jaguar warrior, a man who would give his life for their emperor if necessary.

"Atok....you came," she whispered. And then, Chaska broke into more tears, unable to stop them.

Atok halted, shocked by her weeping. What was wrong? Without thinking, he wrapped his strong arms around her. Chaska was like a fluid reed in his embrace—soft, lithe and so incredibly warm. "Chaska? Why are you weeping?" He held her tightly against him, frightened.

Finally, Chaska gulped back her tears and lifted her face. Atok's broad, strong face filled with concern as she told him, "My grandmother…she's dying…" She began to cry again.

Her wet, hot tears bathed his naked chest. Atok could only hold her, rock her gently in his arms and try to absorb some of her pain and coming loss. His heart ripped open and Atok felt her pain as if it were his own. Yes, as twin flames, they would feel one another's emotions. Allowing his fingers to linger across her strong, silky black hair, he soothed her with his tender caresses. Love tripled inside Atok. In the rare times when he was not refining the powers of his mind and his psychic skills, he dreamed of kissing Chaska. Of asking her to marry him after he survived graduation. Oh, he saw the look in her golden eyes, that innocence, that desire for him. Atok knew he was very handsome. His body had grown and strengthened from the many tests he had been given as a jaguar warrior student. He wanted nothing more than to have the emperor proclaim that Chaska would be his wife after he graduated.

Now, he was in turmoil. In another few minutes, he had to leave or he would be discovered missing by the master teacher. If he was found gone, he would be thrown out of the program, shamed forever. He would not be able to rise above his poor station in life to marry someone as beautiful and sweet as Chaska.

"Listen to me," he whispered urgently next to her ear. "I'm so sorry about your grandmother. I will pray for her. I must leave, Chaska. I cannot be found away from the school. Just know I love you, my beautiful woman. I dream of you nightly. I see your face in the rainbows above Machu Picchu. I cannot live without you, my beloved."

Atok pressed a kiss to her hair and held her tight. Her tears ceased; her breathing was ragged. Chaska was listening to him. Closing his eyes, Atok choked out, "I am going to ask for your hand in marriage when I graduate, beloved. I will request that our emperor give me to you. I love you! I love you with every breath I take...."

Chapter 11

Fox waited tensely. Had the dream he'd sent Aella worked? Did she believe what she saw, that Guerra had possessed Robert? Even though he'd broken a cosmic law, Fox was more than prepared to argue it before the court at the Village of the Clouds. When a spirit or human who was being educated in the great fortress of the Light made a conscious decision to break a law, a jury of peers would convene to decide that individual's punishment.

And he couldn't help himself: he'd had to

send Aella the dream of how they'd finally met and held one another when he was about to graduate from the school. That morning, when he'd stalked her as silently as a jaguar to the Lunar Temple and discovered her crying, had ripped him apart. Atok had fallen helplessly and hopelessly in love with Chaska. She was sweet, innocent, beautiful and above all, his spiritual mate for all time. There were days when all he could feel was the desire to kiss her ripe, full lips. Sending her that dream broke the laws again, but Atok didn't care. Aella had to know his love was eternal. There was such a driving need to connect their past with their present. Aella was not a strong psychic, which worried him. She did not know Victor had possessed Robert. Every moment she spent with the sorcerer, she courted death. Somehow, in desperation, Atok had to protect her. But could he ultimately save her?

Seeing the Toyota pull into the empty parking lot at eight that morning, Fox halted. He couldn't see or tell anything until Aella fully emerged from the car. As she did, his heart fell. *No! Oh, Great Mother, no!* Her aura did not show any wariness or defensiveness toward Robert.

Why didn't Aella believe him? He'd been stark and blunt with the dream information he'd sent to her last night. Peering anxiously, he noticed the dark shadows beneath Aella's eyes. Worse, he saw Guerra had connected an energy line between them. Fox was very sure he wasn't about to suck energy out of her aura, which is what sorcerers did all the time to their victims. That would distract her, and Victor wanted the sphere far more than draining her of energy. They were the true vampires of the cosmos.

Fox had to get Aella's attention but, of course, Victor knew he'd be watching. The sorcerer turned and looked smugly in his direction, silently laughing at him. So long as Guerra remained in the human body, Fox had no right to remove him from this sacred site maintained by the Light. A violent need to kill overwhelmed Fox. Oh, he knew it wasn't the appropriate emotion to have, but at this point, Fox didn't care. As a warrior, he was on the front lines to fight and protect. Now, he could do neither. Frustrated, he followed them as they walked around to the mouth of the serpent mound. Guerra would not bother Aella until she found the sphere—if the sphere was here. He didn't know if it was or not, and thus far, it had not revealed itself.

Today was the full moon and Fox knew the power of that luminary in the sky. Many things would trigger and reveal themselves, for better or worse. That energy would be at its zenith at 10:00 a.m. today. His heart pounded with fear. Fear of the unknown for Aella. For himself. For what Guerra could do and hadn't...yet.

"I'm going to sit here and get ready to travel," Aella told Robert. He stood to one side, notebook in hand. She hadn't slept well after the dream. While she sensed that Fox was nearby, Aella simply didn't have the energy to open up and speak with him. No, when she did

this type of intense work, she had to expend
her energy carefully or she would not meet the
objective.

"I'll go keep watch," Robert said. He smiled
as Aella settled down at the buckeye tree that
sat opposite the snake's mouth. "My gut tells
me that you'll find the emerald sphere today."

"I hope you're right," Aella said smoothing
out the towel beneath her.

"You okay?"

"Yes, just a little short on sleep last night."
She almost told Robert about the dream, but
decided not to. The other dream had soothed
her worries. How could it not? Atok had asked
her hand in marriage. Aella felt the sadness
of her grandmother dying and the euphoria of
Atok loving her from afar.

Sighing, Aella needed to stay on point with
their mission. Robert seemed well-rested, as
virile as usual and as handsome. Yet, Aella
still felt the confusing mix of energy around
him. His aura had moved from the clear colors

it used to have to more muddied colors. "Are you feeling okay, Robert?"

"Yes, of course." Guerra kept his feelings shielded from Aella. She gave him a quizzical look, as if not believing him. The amount of energy it took to keep Robert's spirit in check was huge. Victor had not expected the man's spirit would be so powerful for so long. Usually, a possessed spirit fought initially but then surrendered. Not Robert's. Last night, Guerra had almost cut the silver cord to release the bastard's spirit so that he could take over the body completely.

"Your aura..."

"Oh, that. Yes, I'm fighting a bit of a stomach bug," he lied. "Maybe it was the shrimp I ate two nights ago." He saw her frown ease. Good, she'd bought the lie.

"That's it," Aella murmured. "I was worried about you."

"That's sweet of you, but really, I'm okay." He smiled warmly down at her.

Aella settled her back against the trunk of

the tree. Her legs were drawn upward close to her body. "Okay, I'm going in."

"Go for it," Robert urged. "I'll be nearby." He watched as her eyes closed. His anger over Robert's fighting spirit was enough. Stepping away, Guerra moved to where Aella could not see him. The July morning was warm and humid, typical for this time of year. The sun's rays slanted upward and would crest the tops of the trees in another hour. Robins hopped around on the serpent mound looking for worms in the recently cut grass. A great blue heron flew overhead.

Victor had a choice to make. If Aella found the sphere, he would need all his energy to steal it from her. Right now, Robert took about forty percent of his energy. He couldn't just cut the silver cord on the bastard because Victor needed his knowledge. What if Aella didn't find the sphere this morning? If Victor cut the cord on Robert would he still be able to maintain his cover with her? There were dangers here and Victor knew all of them.

Robert's aura was key. If he got rid of the archeologist's spirit, the aura would change to Victor's. Then Aella could see the dramatic change in colors. Would she note the difference? After all, she was weak in the psychic department. Victor seriously wondered if Aella was trained in possession at all. She hadn't sensed him attacking Robert, and anyone trained would surely have known what was going on. She had not. Feeling smug, Victor decided Aella was no threat at all. He would play his hand as he saw fit.

Standing there, he glanced toward the parking lot. No tourists had arrived yet; they were alone, and that was good. Guerra didn't want anyone around if Aella stumbled upon the sphere. Chewing over his problems, Victor knew that if Aella did not find the sphere this morning, it meant future days with her. She was always asking questions in regards to the archeology of the area. If he cut Robert loose, Victor would have to start making up things on the fly.

Victor sensed she'd find the sphere today. He saw Fox, the jaguar warrior, hovering near her. When their eyes met, Victor smiled. The Incan warrior hated him with a passion that transcended any earthly emotion. Used to such hatred from the Warriors for the Light, Victor shrugged it off.

What to do? Guerra made a decision. He cut the silver cord on Robert's spirit. Pushing the freed spirit of the archeologist out the top of the crown chakra, Victor watched him move upward and then disappear into the light.

Good riddance… Victor sighed and felt the internal pressure within the physical body disappear.

Standing there, he allowed the physical body to get used to only having one inhabitant. He summoned Lothar, his knight, to the mound area. Almost instantly, he saw the *Tupay* standing just outside the boundary.

Lothar, I believe she will find the sphere. Stand by, I may need help. This Warrior for the Light is more than ready to pounce on

me, but he cannot so long as I'm in this body,
Victor said.

I understand, my lord. I will await your in-structions.

Fox felt panic as he watched the knight from
the *Tupay* appear just feet away from the protective boundary. Worse, he'd seen Robert's
spirit shoot out of the top of his head and leave.
Guerra had cut the cord. Robert was now of-
ficially dead for this lifetime. Fox was how
outnumbered, and for once, he wished Chima
were here. He'd already sent an alarming message telepathically to the Village of the Clouds,
begging Alaria and Adaire for reinforcements.
Something was about to happen and Fox knew
he couldn't handle it all by himself.

All his focus was on Aella. If Guerra
wanted to he could possess her body. If he did,
she would die five minutes after he left her.
That couldn't happen! He felt panic as never
before and yet, he was helpless. Aella did not
have the ability to focus her psychic energy on

more than one thing. And right now, she was astrally exploring the cave beneath the head of the snake. All he could do was wait, watch and pray.

Aella stood in the yellow and white limestone cave beneath the head of the snake. As she began to look around, her goddess, Athena, materialized before her. Shocked by the unexpected visit, Aella bowed to her.

My lady, she greeted. *I'm surprised by your visit. Is something wrong?*

Athena, in her usual garb, stood with her barn owl on the left shoulder and the Medusa shield sitting on the ground, her right hand upon the top of it. *Aella, you must be careful. There is a spider in your midst who is weaving a deadly web. Be alert...*

Stunned by the warning, Aella watched the goddess fade away. She knew she had to be careful, but this seemed dire. How she wished her gifts were more extensive so that she could see the road ahead. All she could do was to keep searching for the sphere. Mystified, a little fearful, Aella became even more careful in her investigation of the cave. She saw a number of spiders with webs in this cave, much more than in the others. Perhaps her goddess was warning her not to get bitten by one of them? Shaking her head, Aella felt a bit of comic relief as she peered around the wall. Athena always talked in mystifying generalities. But then, the goddess couldn't tell her bluntly what to be wary of.

As Aella moved around just above the nubby texture of the floor, the light seem to infuse a particular spiderweb on the opposite wall. It was a stunning one, perfectly round with thirty or so concentric circles woven into it. Drawn to the structure, Aella gasped in surprise. As she stepped over to admire its beauty, she noticed another altar. It, too, was about four feet tall and had been hidden behind a fold in the cave's wall.

As on the other altar, each of the sedimentary rocks in its construction were of ochre and cream colors and had been lovingly hand-hewn and rounded. The symbols were different on this one from those she'd seen on the alter under the egg yesterday. Kneeling down before the altar, she placed her fingers on several of the smoothed stones. The other altar had had at least fifteen animal symbols carved into various stones.

It was not so on this altar. Instead, each stone was carved with a figure 8 turned sideways. It was the vesica pisces symbol! Gasping, Aella realized the significance of this particular, ageless symbol. This was the symbol of the Emerald Key necklace! Each of the other spheres that had been retrieved had letters carved into one side. On the opposite side was emblazoned the vesica pisces symbol.

Heart beginning to pound, she understood that the emerald sphere must be here. Excitement rose with trepidation within her as she ran her fingers across the stones and the symbol. Was the sphere here? If so, where? Were the stones arranged in such a way that they had to be touched in a specific order? Unsure, Aella looked up. The spiderweb seemed to shimmer with rainbow colors. The spider at the center, to her surprise, had a red vesica pisces symbol on her black abdomen. Thinking at first it was a black widow, Aella realized with a start that this was no common spider.

As soon as she made that connection, the spider moved quickly up her web to the left upper quadrant. There, she thrummed her body so that it looked as if she was bouncing up and down on a trampoline. Aella tried to understand what the spirit spider was trying to tell her.

Gazing down at the altar, she perused the stones. The cave light was not bright, and she had to get much closer to peer at the stones in the upper left quadrant of the altar. As her fingers touched a larger cream-colored stone, electricity leaped into her fingers. Instantly, the stone began to glow.

Yelping, Aella jerked her fingers away. It had felt like a mild shock, a tingling, wild and warm feeling. Excitedly, she watch the stone glow golden. It pulsated, like a beating heart. Anxiously, she looked to the spider in her web above the altar.

The spider move back down to the center of her web and then scuttled quickly up to the upper right quadrant. Again, she vibrated her body. Aella nodded and looked closely at the altar's right upper quadrant. She hesitantly placed her hands on an ochre stone that appeared larger than the others. Again, that spark of energy leaped from the rock to her fingers. As she jerked her hand back, that rock began to pulsate and glow.

Amazed, Aella understood what was going on. The spider was the doorkeeper to the emerald sphere. It was no accident that her beautiful web was above the center of the altar. She watched the spider dash down to the lower left quadrant. This time, she boldly placed her fingers on that pale-yellow stone. Again, the tingling occurred but she didn't jerk away. As she removed her fingers, that stone began to glow.

Sitting back on her heels, Aella saw the three stones continuing to pulsate in rhythm with one another. Amazed and humbled by the spectacle, she looked to the spider for direction. Athena had a spider who helped her weave. Was this her spider? Is this why the goddess had appeared? Unsure, Aella watched the spider quickly move to the center and then back to the lower right quadrant.

Smiling, she crouched down to see the fourth rock in that position. Touching it, the tingles flying wildly up her hand, she saw that rock, too, glow and pulse. The spider quickly moved back to the center of her web where she vigorously leaped up and down.

Okay, Aella thought, *the fifth stone must be in the center of the altar.* An ochre stone sat in the center. Was this the one to touch? She reached out, and her fingertips connected with the stone. Aella wasn't prepared for what happened next.

As she made contact with it, the entire cave lit up with a pale-green energy. It seemed to emanate from the altar. The energy within the cave changed remarkably and a feeling of intense love swirled in and around her as she got to her feet. It drove tears of gratitude to Aella's eyes.

The web of the spider became lost in the deepening green color that now flowed to the top of the altar. Aella watched as the five stones glowed brighter and then more dully. It was as if there was some mathematical precision known only to the stones themselves.

Aella gasped as the emerald sphere slowly emerged from within the altar and hovered inches above. No longer was there a spider or a web. Just the clear, incredible beauty of a golf-ball-sized emerald sphere. Aella felt shock, pleasure and amazement. The golden and green shafts of light shooting out of the sphere were like a sun blazing within the cavern.

Heart swelling with humility, Aella felt the connection of the spirit of the sphere with her. She bowed her head and telepathed, *I am honored by your appearance, dear spirit.*

As am I, daughter of the Light. Come forward and pick me up.

Aella felt giddy as she slid her hand gently beneath the sphere. Mesmerized by its beauty, by the profound love that emanated from it, she realized instantly why the Vesica Pisces Foundation wanted the necklace. Absorbing the intense love, Aella felt renewed, lifted and a part of something so great and profound that words could never do it justice.

Tell me dear spirit, what is inscribed upon you? What does the word mean? Aella asked.

Daughter of the Light, I am honesty. Without truth in the All, there is heavy energy and darkness. Truth frees each being to walk the path toward Oneness and Light.

Thank you for your wise words. May I take you from this cave?

Yes, I must begin my journey, the sphere answered.

Aella knew that as she left the mound, the energy of the sphere would go with her. She floated out of the cave and back into the third dimension. The moment she did, shafts of powerful green and gold blazed out into the third-dimensional world. She was bathed with the colors but focused on getting back into her body and grounding it into the here and now.

Fox gasped as he saw Aella's astral body rise out of the mound, the emerald sphere resting in her right hand. He'd heard about the spheres because it had been his emperor who'd had the vision to create them. Now, as the emerald and gold rays bathed him, he understood their importance. There was a loving sensation, so warm and enduring, that for a moment, it erased Fox's trepidation and panic. As he saw Aella slide back into her physical body, he felt a puncturing energy, much like a jet breaking the sound barrier.

Whirling around, he saw Guerra in Robert's body, running around the mound, his face filled with naked greed. What was he going to do?

Chapter 12

Aella sat with the emerald sphere pulsing in her left hand. She was completing the process of returning into her body when she felt the hard grip of Robert's hand on her arm.

"Get up!" he snapped, hauling her to her feet.

"Robert?" Aella tried to wrest her arm from his grip. She looked into his face. It was grim, his eyes focused on her. "What's wrong?"

"We have to get out of here now. Hold on to the sphere."

Confused, Aella held the sphere tightly as he yanked her forward, nearly causing her to fall.

"You're hurting me!" Aella cried. She fought the dizziness that always came with returning to her physical body. "Why are you doing this? There's nothing wrong." This time, she jerked her arm out of his hand. She started to feel afraid and looked around for help.

Turning, Victor glared at her. He could take the sphere out of her hand, but it might disappear. Would the sphere remain in a *Tupay*'s hand or not? Victor simply didn't know. The conservative decision would be to have Aella hold it until he got her beyond the sacred energy of this mound. Then, Victor could snatch it out of her hand. The sphere would not disappear on him then. "There's danger. We've got to leave here immediately, Aella," he snarled through gritted teeth. His arm snaked out and he grabbed her again. One way or another, Victor would get that sphere! If he had to drag Aella screaming out of here across that boundary to where Lothar waited, he'd do it.

Gasping, Aella screamed, "No! What's got into you?" She yanked away from his large hand. He seemed so different from the man she'd met so recently. His eyes were a flat black, narrowed upon her, with hatred in them. This was not the Robert she knew.

"Oh, no!" She realized with a jolt that Victor had possessed Robert's body. This explained all the confusing things she'd seen in him the past few days. Aella panicked. If he could get her beyond the protection of this sacred site, he would take the sphere.

Without the necessary power to stop Robert, she felt alone. He cursed and lunged at her. On instinct, Aella turned on her heel, dug the toes of her tennis shoes into the soft grass and ran. Her mind whirled with questions. Could she get the security guard's attention? Couldn't Fox help her? He knew how important the sphere was to the Light. Breath tore out of her mouth as she wove in and out of the trees down the hill. Hearing Robert's large footfalls coming up on her, Aella tried to think what to do.

Fox saw the drama playing out. Unless Victor was beyond the boundary, there was little he could do to protect Aella. He watched her running like a deer in flight toward the mouth of the serpent. Fox moved into action and did what he could. Victor was gaining on her and in a few seconds, he would grab her. And then what? The sorcerer would have no qualms about killing Aella to get the sphere.

Grimly, Fox used his energy to trip Robert. He moved a branch from a fallen tree in front of him. With an "oomph," Robert crashed to the ground. It gave Aella some time. But not much.

Cursing, Victor saw the Warrior for the Light hovering in front of him. *Bastard!* he hurled at him. Rage filled the sorcerer. In a physical body his own energies were lowered. If he were in spirit, he could hurl energy as powerful as a lightning bolt at this guardian. But in body, he could not or he'd fry the physical form and he'd be at the mercy of the sacred Light energy.

Leave her alone! The sphere is hers, not yours! Fox telepathed, standing in his way.

Robert laughed harshly. *Go away, piss ant! That sphere is mine!* Lunging upward, Victor drove the body to its feet and raced up the hill toward the fleeing Aella. Huffing, he sprang up and over several fallen logs and reached out. He grabbed at Aella's yellow T-shirt. He had her!

Aella screamed as she was yanked off her feet. She tumbled end over end with Victor. Twigs and debris exploded around them and the air was knocked out of her. Victor sprang to his feet first. His hand splayed out across her chest and kept her down on the ground. Victor had had enough of this foolishness and decided to take the sphere. It was a risky move, but he had no other choice. Aella was fighting back too much and he had no other strategy.

"Give it to me!" Victor hissed, trying to grab her hand. Aella screamed and tried to push him off, but she was no match for his weight. In an instant, Victor snagged her hand.

Fox hurled energy from his palms. The white light shot out like a bolt coming out of the blue toward Robert. The sorcerer was lifted off Aella in a split second. He flew through the air and landed heavily in the woodlands, tumbling over and over until he slammed into the trunk of a huge buckeye.

Aella gasped. She realized belatedly that Fox had somehow helped her. Now, she had a chance to make a run for the car! Once she got into it, she was safe! Gripping the sphere protectively in her left hand, she leaped to her feet and sprinted toward the parking lot.

Victor shook his head as he watched Aella bound like a graceful deer out of the woodlands. In an instant, he realized she was going to try and make it to the car. She had the car keys, dammit! Grunting, his physical body stunned, Victor pushed it to the max. The bolt of energy Fox had released at him had been enough to kill a mere mortal, but he was immortal. Victor kept tripping, the human form still in shock from the energy blow delivered by the guardian. Cursing over and over, Victor forced the human being in hot pursuit of Aella.

Aella burst out onto the asphalt. The car was only a hundred feet away! Gasping hard, she tried to find the keys for it in her right pocket. Behind her, she heard the heavy breathing of Robert. Could Fox help her now? She didn't know.

With a cry, Aella saw the keys fly out of her fingers. They hit the asphalt in front of the Toyota. Leaning down, she picked them up.

Robert struck.

Fox left the sacred site.

He knew that by doing this, he was breaking a law that would carry serious penalties. But he didn't care. He had to save Aella!

The sorcerer threw her against the car. When she slammed into the Toyota, the sphere flew out of her hand. In one second, Victor grabbed the sphere in midair. As his hand closed about it, triumph soared through him.

Aella screamed. She launched herself at Robert as he caught the emerald sphere. Knowing how important it was to have the emerald, she struck him with all her strength. She pummeled his face and neck, throwing him backward and off balance.

But Victor laughed and pulled out of Robert's body. Immediately, the archeologist's physical form collapsed to the pavement. Aella stumbled, horrified as she looked down at Robert's unmoving form.

Victor hovered above the body and waited for his help. Lothar came quickly. The Dark Lord handed his knight the sphere. *Take it to the castle. There, no warrior can get to it. I have business to finish with this bitch. Now, leave!*

Victor watched Lothar blink out of the third dimension. Satisfied that sphere was in safe hands, he refocused his hatred on Aella, who was standing over the body of the human. He would possess her, leave and let her die, too. That would be two less Warriors for the Light to have to battle in the future.

From a safe distance Fox saw the Dark Lord's intent. He had no time to think. Aella's life was at stake and the emerald sphere was gone. Without thinking, Fox slammed into Robert's body. If he possessed it within a five-minute limit, he could own it. By doing so, he was damning himself to mortality, but he didn't care. Aella's life was too important to protect. Victor could destroy her in one blast as she stood looking down at Robert.

Aella saw Robert's eyes open. His face was grayish from death and suddenly, it flooded with life again. Leaping back, she couldn't contain her shock. She was both paralyzed and desperate to act.

Fox forced the body of the archeologist to stand. He saw Victor coming toward Aella, his eyes glowing red with malevolent intent. He was going to kill her.

Not if he could help it. With Robert's heavy

body around him, Fox marshaled every bit of
energy that was his to possess. Holding up his
hands, palms out and aimed at the dark, roiling
black cloud coming toward him. Fox anchored
himself in the body.

Victor had never seen a guardian possess
a human before. Warriors for the Light did
not do this! Only the *Tupay*! He hadn't even
known it was possible. Stunned, Victor took
precious seconds to think through this unexpected occurrence. The human body of Robert
Cramer looked just as alive as when Victor had
possessed it. Shaking his head, Victor returned
his focus to the woman who stood feet behind
the Incan guardian.

What did this mean? Did the guardian still
have his powers? Cursing the Great Mother,
Victor brought all his energy to bear within his
spirit. He was like a nuclear power station now,
and as he loosed a double charge of energy toward Aella, he saw the guardian lift the hands
of the human to stop his attack.

Victor laughed. His energy would fry the

human form, would more than likely destroy
the spirit of the guardian and would kill Aella
to boot. With savage intent, Victor hurled it at
them.

Fox saw the twin charges release from the
black cloud of the sorcerer. In that moment, he
was prepared to die so that Aella could live.
His heart swelled with the power of love that
soared in all directions. As the charges struck
his palms, Fox felt the white-hot heat drive
through the human body. He expected to die.

But that did not happen. To his shock, Fox
saw the beams striking his palms and then re-
flecting back toward Victor!

Victor yelped in surprise. His own bolts of
energy would have killed him instead, but he
acted quickly and blinked out of the third dimension in order to avoid being hit by them.
Without looking back, the sorcerer, laughing, quickly made his way back to the castle
of the *Tupay* in the fourth dimension. There,
he would be safe. Just as no one from the
Tupay could ever break into the Village of

the Clouds, the reverse was true: no *Taqe* or Warrior for the Light was ever allowed into the *Tupay* fortress.

Filled with glee, Victor swiftly made his way home. Lothar would have the vaunted emerald sphere. At last, after three tries, he had one of the spheres. And without all of them, the *Taqe* could not restring the emerald necklace and use it to shift the energy toward Light instead of the heavy energy of darkness. He had won! His people would celebrate mightily now.

Aella watched in horrified fascination. She saw the dark cloud that had condensed so that no one could see it. It appeared to be a momentary thunderstorm that had suddenly appeared above them. When Robert had held his palms outward and braced himself, she didn't understand his reaction. When the twin bolts of energy released from the roiling storm, it was Robert who took the hit and reflected the energy back at the cloud. In less than a split second, the dark, angry cloud disappeared before her eyes.

Robert staggered back a few feet. When he fell to his knees, his hands gripping his chest, she didn't know what to do. Was Victor still inside him? Should she run for the car? Something told her to wait. Heart pounding, Aella realized how close to death she'd come. But if Victor was still in Robert's body, he would shake off whatever had sent him to his knees and come after her again.

Fox tried with all his might to recover from the sorcerer's charge. He felt Aella nearby. She was safe! That was all he cared about. Placing his hands on the asphalt, he tried to dissolve the energy still coursing through the body. How odd it felt to be back into human form. Fox had forgotten how heavy it felt around his spirit, as if he were wearing armor.

Opening his mouth, he gasped for air, unable to speak. How his heart seemed to thud out of his chest. The first sensation—Aella's wariness.

He picked up her disjointed thoughts telepathically. She was grateful Robert was alive. So was he since he hadn't thought he would survive the sorcerer's attack. Looking around, he noticed Victor Guerra had left. Why wouldn't he? He had what he wanted: the sphere.

Severe nausea flowed through Fox. He vomited until he went into dry heaves. His extremities shook and all he could do was kneel, allowing the contents in the man's stomach to spew out of him. The physical body had taken a hit even though he'd been able to deflect most of the sorcerer's energy. This was the aftermath of such an attack.

Above all, Fox wanted Aella to realize that the sorcerer wasn't in this body. Wiping his mouth, his eyes watering, he weakly turned his head. "Aella, it's me, Fox. The sorcerer is gone. You're safe…safe…." And he fainted.

A stab of pain brought Fox from unconsciousness. The sterile smell of alcohol filled his nose and he frowned.

"Robert?"

Aella's soft, urgent voice registered. Where was he? Fox forced open his eyes. What he saw made his heart leap with joy.

Aella was leaning over him. Her soft black hair curled about her head, her golden eyes were anxious. It was the parting of her soft lips that made him groan. Her warm fingers touched his shoulder.

"Robert? You're in a Dayton, Ohio, hospital. The security guard at the serpent mound called the EMTs. You've been unconscious for twenty-four hours." Aella looked up. The beeps and shrieks of the machines were considerable. They had placed him in ICU. On the way in the ambulance, the paramedics had said they couldn't steady Robert's heartbeat. It was erratic and they thought for sure he'd have a heart attack. But he hadn't. At least, not yet.

Anxiously, Aella searched his eyes. As she spoke softly to him, her fingers grazing his shoulder, she watched the pupils enlarge and focus on her. "Robert? Fox?" The corners of his strong mouth curved very slightly upward.

"Chaska..."

That was all Aella needed. She knew from the dream Fox had originally sent her, that that had been her name when she was his wife in the time of the Incas in Peru. "Ohhh..." she sighed, closing her eyes for a moment and gripping his shoulder more firmly. "Thank goodness..." Aella felt a sense of hope. The doctors had said they didn't know what was wrong with Robert except that his heart was beating erratically, and they couldn't get it to settle down. They'd warned her that he would probably die. It was only a matter of time. "Fox?"

"Yes, beloved..." he managed in a hoarse whisper.

Looking up, she saw the women at the nurses' station taking an interest in Fox becoming conscious. "Listen, your heartbeat is erratic. They say they can't regulate the rhythm. Can you do anything to get it back to normal, Fox?" Her voice tightened and she clung to his gaze. "I don't want you to die. The doctors say you will. Please, Fox…if there's anything you can do…?"

Nodding very slightly, Fox closed his eyes. As a guardian, he knew how to adjust a human body's various systems. Of course, Fox had never thought he'd be doing it for himself. Right now, he knew he was in supreme trouble with the leaders from the Village of the Clouds. He'd done something a *Tupay* would do: possess a body. *Taqe* never did that. But he'd had to—to save his beloved one's life. Fox had no qualms about his decision. Just knowing he'd saved Aella's life was all Fox cared about.

Within five minutes, he normalized all the functions within the human vehicle. Now, he would begin to heal. The charge released by Guerra would stay no more than forty-eight hours within the physical form. It would dissipate after having done its damage. Fortunately for Fox, he had the power to stop ninety-nine percent of the blast. The destructive symptoms tapered off and now he would fully recover.

A nurse came in. "He's conscious?"

Aella nodded and stepped aside. "Yes."

The nurse smiled down at the man. "Mr. Cramer, can you hear me? I'm Wanda Starling. You're in the ICU unit and I'm taking care of you."

Fox opened his eyes. The registered nurse was in her forties, with short red hair and merry blue eyes. He liked her smile. "Nice to meet you," he said in a hoarse voice. "I'm thirsty. And I'm hungry."

With a slight laugh, the nurse shook her head as she studied the monitors. "This is amazing, Mr. Cramer. Your heartbeat is normal!" She gestured to several of the instruments surrounding his bed. "Everything looks normal. Let me get your cardiologist Dr. Susan Levi. If she approves, I can get you off the IV, give you some ice chips, and get you some food if she thinks you're ready to eat."

For the next hour, Fox endured the comings

and goings of several doctors and nurses, made palatable by the fact that Aella sat in the small ICU unit, just a hand's touch away from him. Everyone who came in shook their heads in amazement. Dr. Levi, an energetic young woman of around thirty-five was shocked by his sudden recovery. She kept listening to his heart with her stethoscope, ordered up a test to look at his heart. Everything came back normal.

"Mr. Cramer," Dr. Levi said as she came back to the ICU unit, "you are a miracle. Every lab test and ultrasound we performed on your heart came back normal." She took the chart and scribbled on it with her black pen. "I'm releasing you from ICU but I want you to stay with us one more day just to make sure. I'll have you transferred to another floor. You can have all the fluids and food you want." Giving him a smile, she patted his shoulder. "Welcome back to the land of the living, Mr. Cramer."

Chapter 13

Aella took a deep breath as she switched off the GPS phone. Standing outside the hospital, the July sunlight warming her, she felt utterly defeated. She had talked with Calen at the Vesica Pisces Foundation and told her she'd lost the sphere, and the weight of what had transpired had settled heavily on her shoulders. She tucked the large phone back into her attaché case and sat on the bench beneath the massive buckeye trees.

People came and went from the Dayton hospital. Looking around, she pushed her damp palms along her jeans. Everything was topsy-turvy. Nothing had gone as planned. How had she lost the sphere? She'd never forget the disappointment in Calen's voice, and she herself felt it on all levels. After having held the emerald sphere, connected with it, she understood just how vital it was to the necklace. Now, she had lost the fourth of the seven spheres. Their mission had failed.

Worse, Robert was dead. Victor Guerra had cut the silver cord to the archeologist's spirit. Grief wound its way up from her chest. Tears came and Aella cried for his loss. He had been a good man. Oh, a touch arrogant, but he had never failed to be kind or help her during the mission. Guerra had savagely attacked and possessed his body and she hadn't even known it had taken place.

Hands pressed to her face, Aella sobbed over her own failings. Calen and Reno had hired her precisely because she was clairvoyant. Why hadn't she seen Victor? In reality,

Aella's training had not prepared her for combat against sorcerers. Sniffing, she pulled a tissue from her purse and wiped her eyes and blew her nose. There was no sense in feeling sorry for herself.

Calen and Reno would arrive tomorrow morning. They wanted to speak to Fox, the *Taqe* warrior who had taken over Robert's body. Now that he was stable, perhaps Fox could shed light on events that Aella could not. Hands in her lap, the tissue in her fist, Aella remembered that Athena had appeared twice to warn her of things to come, warnings that were vague, general and non-specific.

Well, she'd failed. Utterly. Robert was dead. The emerald sphere was gone. And no one, no *Taqe*, could ever go to the bastion of the *Tupay* and retrieve it. Her mind churned over the fact she'd lost it to Guerra.

Aella glanced up at the five-story hospital. Fox had been transferred to a private room on the second floor. She should go see him. Aella had left the hospital in a taxi last night and gone to the Marriott Hotel in downtown Dayton. She'd slept deeply. A refreshing warm shower had washed away most of the drugged feeling she'd had since the confrontation with Guerra. Aella suspected her own aura was toxic with the energy of the fight in which Fox had protected her from certain death.

Pushing her fingers through her softly curling hair, Aella forced herself to stand up. It was time to visit Fox but she still felt vulnerable and unsure. So much had happened. She could feel Fox worrying about her. It was as if they were connected to one another telepathically whether Aella wanted it or not.

She stepped through the doors and took the stairs to the second floor. The clock on the wall of the busy nurses' station read 10:00 a.m. The door to room 205 was closed. Gently, she twisted the door handle and pushed it open enough to peek in.

"Come in," Fox called. His heart leaped and then pounded to underscore Aella's visit. She looked fetching in a pale-green T-shirt, jeans that showed off her long, lovely legs and a pair of burgundy leather sandals. Seeing the darkness beneath her eyes, Fox was all too aware of her present emotional state of dishevelment.

Aella quietly closed the door and walked over to his bed. Fox was still in a light-blue hospital gown but it couldn't hide his broad shoulders and massive chest. "How are you doing?" she asked, her voice soft as she set her attaché case on the floor next to the bed.

"Better," Fox said. He watched as she picked up a chair and brought it over to the bed. How badly he wanted to crush Aella in his arms, kiss and hold her. Yet, everything within him screamed against it. Because they were from the same soul, Fox could access her feelings and thoughts. Right now, she was distracted, confused and unsure of her feelings toward him. Fox understood.

Pulling up the chair, Aella sat down, hands in her lap. She searched his face. "You look stronger. Are you?"

"Very much so. You look tired. What

happened?" Fox stopped himself from reaching out to touch her pale cheek. Aella seemed devastated.

She relayed her conversation with Calen. "I failed. It's not a good feeling. The emerald sphere was so much more than me or you...it was for the good of this planet."

Fox couldn't stop himself. He sat up and leaned over, his hand resting gently on her shoulder. "Aella, what happened was not your fault. I've been going over this situation in my mind and there were real problems with the mission itself."

His hand was warm, even comforting to Aella. She greedily absorbed his unexpected touch like a starving beggar. Shocked by her own level of neediness, she suddenly realized that since the confrontation, she'd wanted to be held. Just for a little bit. It wouldn't change the outcome, but she'd feel better. Tucking her lower lip between her teeth, she said nothing. When Fox removed his hand, she wanted to cry.

Fox was slammed with the need. Should he? Aella still looked at him strangely; perhaps she was still adapting to the fact that Robert was gone and he was here, in his place. Never before had Fox understood the law about not possessing a body until now. He wondered starkly if he could lose Aella. That thought shattered him. Yet, as he sat there, arms around his drawn-up legs, Fox realized it could happen. Aella was devastated by the unexpected turn of events. She had liked Robert. And if he hadn't interfered as he had, she might have fallen in love with him over time. Now, Robert was gone, and Fox owned his body instead. Could Aella learn to love him all over again? Could she see Robert's face and body but know Fox was in there? He began to realize the enormity of such a task.

Fox digested the warnings from his training, the laws in place and Alaria's words. Now he was living the end result of his decisions, Fox saw why those laws existed. As much as he loved Chaska, his choices could cost him something he did not want to lose: her love.

"It will be good to speak to Calen and Reno," he told her finally. "I'm sure they're disappointed."

"So am I," Aella muttered glumly. "It was all my fault."

"No," Fox said, his voice stronger and firm. "You did your job. Robert was incapable of doing his. He was the weak link in this mission, not you."

Frowning, she searched his features. How tough it was to see Robert but realize his spirit was gone. "What are you saying, Fox?"

Heartened that she used his name, he said, "Robert was a shape-shifter. He was the wrong person to choose for this mission, Aella. A shape-shifter can change from one form to another, but what good is that against someone like Guerra? You can see he did not have the psychic awareness you had. Have you asked yourself what might have happened if he did? He might have seen Guerra. You cannot be faulted in this, Aella. You did everything asked of you. Calen and Reno expected you to find the sphere and you did. Robert left your flank open to Guerra. He was not as psychic as you and, therefore, was blind when he needed most to see."

Turning the fervently spoken argument over in her mind, Aella shook her head. "But, they needed him, Fox. He was the expert and he had information about that period of time."

"And their decision to use him left you open to attack," Fox said as gently as he could, though Aella still seemed confused. "Listen to me. Calen and Reno chose the wrong person to go with you. They should have sent someone who could see into the fourth dimension like you. If that had happened, I don't think the sorcerer would have been able to pull off the possession of Robert. As it was, you had only so much energy for your job and you couldn't use it to full capacity for other things. If you had, you'd have seen Guerra possess Robert's body."

"That's true, I was really being careful with my energy that morning. Astral travel takes everything out of me."

"That's right," Fox said. He risked everything and tenderly touched her shoulder for just a moment. "Robert was blind-sided, Aella. You cannot take the burden of what happened solely on your own shoulders. Reno and Calen made a bad decision in choosing your partner. Strategically, Robert left you vulnerable. He is not to be blamed in this. The real fault is pointed at the foundation who hired you."

Aella digested Fox's fervent explanation. "I hadn't even thought about any of this."

"Of course you wouldn't. You're devastated by Robert's death and the loss of the sphere."

Giving him a warm look, Aella whispered, "Thanks for understanding."

In that moment, though he was still feeling weak, Fox yearned to wrap his arms around Aella, crush her to his chest and simply hold her. "You're carrying the load for everyone, Aella. That is not right or fair. You're the only one in this mess that did it right. You should feel good that you performed up to their expectations."

"Are you going to discuss this with Reno and Calen when they arrive?" Aella wondered how they would take Fox's assessment of the failed mission.

"Of course I am," Fox said. "I'm not going to allow them to blame you for it."

"It doesn't matter, Fox. We've failed, regardless."

Holding up his hand, he said, "Wait. That is not true. Calen and Reno need to know what they did wrong so that they can fix it for the next team. If they don't learn from their mistakes, they could lose another sphere, not to mention their team. No, if they are the people I believe they are, they will take responsibility. I'm sure they will want to learn how to fix their mistake in time for the next mission."

Nodding, Aella said with a some hope in her tone, "You're a wonderful person, Fox. I was so stuck in the mire of what happened that I didn't see any of this."

"Aella, I love you. You are my life, my breath, my very being. I know you need time to adjust to me…. And I hope you can over time. I will do anything I can to protect and support you," Fox told her in a low quavering tone.

Calen and Reno Manchahi stood grimly around Fox's bed the next morning. Aella sat in a chair after having relayed to them once again everything that had happened with the sphere. "And that's all I can add," Aella said softly, "except to say I'm very, very sorry that we failed on this mission."

Calen nodded sympathetically toward Aella. "In truth, Reno and I have been looking at why we asked Robert Cramer to be on the team in the first place." She traded a quick look with her husband. "We screwed up, Aella. We should have gotten someone with far more clairvoyant experience than Robert.

This wasn't his fault." She touched her chest. "It was ultimately our fault. So, we don't want you to carry the load on this. It's our load, instead."

Fox nodded and was pleased that the humans took responsibility for their actions. "I had told Aella that much yesterday," he informed them.

"You saw it all, Fox?" Calen asked.

"I did. I was very worried. I'm sorry Robert was detached from this life and you have lost the sphere." He gave Aella a tender glance. "At least I was able to save her."

Reno frowned. "We're glad you did, Fox, but you're going to pay a heavy price for your actions."

Smiling slightly, Fox held the Apache's dark stare. "I'm aware of my choices and I'm at peace with them."

Calen shook her head, her hand resting on her hip. "I didn't know that a *Taqe* could possess a human."

"I didn't either," Reno said.

"If you read the Akashic Records," Fox told them, "in the past, we did. At a certain point in our spiritual development, we stopped because it was wrong. We can still do it to this day if we choose to. We never lost the ability to possess."

"Has anyone from the Village of the Clouds visited you yet?" Calen wondered.

Shaking his head, Fox said, "No, but I expect a visit soon."

Aella felt the dread in the room. "I don't understand…" she told them. "If Fox hadn't possessed Robert's dying body, I'd be dead right now. You all seem to feel it was a bad choice on Fox's part to do that."

Calen said, "Aella, you haven't had the advanced training all *Taqe* receive sooner or later. Grandmother Alaria and Grandfather Adaire are the leaders of the Village of the Clouds. That is our fortress of the Light. I know you have had training through the goddess Athena, whom you serve. There are so many cosmic rules to adhere to when you're walking the path of Light. Fox made a free-will choice to ignore one of those laws in order to save you from dying at Guerra's hands."

Staring at Fox, Aella asked, "Then, what you did was wrong?" The incredulity in her voice resonated around the room.

Fox reached out and held her hand for a moment. "Don't concern yourself with this, Aella. I will deal with Alaria and Adaire when the time comes."

Fear clogged her throat. "What does it all mean, Fox? If you did something wrong, can they punish you?"

Fox squeezed her hand. "Aella, nothing is going to happen to me. Now, stop worrying. You've been through enough." He gave Calen and Reno a warning look that spoke volumes. "We're done talking about me. I'm not what is important. The loss of the sphere should be our focus."

Her hand tingled in the wake of his contact. Every time Fox touched her, Aella felt her heart open up just a bit more to him, though she still wrestled with the fact it was Robert's body with a different spirit inside it. "Okay," she said. Fox did not look perturbed at all. Calen and Reno clearly did. If Fox wasn't concerned about it, Aella wasn't going to be, either.

"What plans do you have to try and retrieve the stolen sphere?" Fox asked them.

Reno shrugged. "We have none. When we get back to Quito, Ecuador, to the foundation headquarters, we'll go to the Village of the Clouds and speak to Alaria and Adaire. From our perspective and knowledge, nothing can be done."

"That's right," Calen added sorrowfully. "We're hoping that Alaria and Adaire can give us strategy or ideas first of all on how to find it and then steal it back."

Fox felt their sadness over the situation. "Nothing in any dimension is ever straightforward," he reminded them. "There are always obstacles."

Calen smiled a little. "Aella said you were

a jaguar warrior with Emperor Pachacuti in your last physical incarnation. I imagine the psychic training you got there has served you very well."

Nodding, Fox said, "Yes, it did. That is why I can tell you not to feel defeated about losing this sphere. If anything, this mission will help you choose better people for the next one. When you go after something this important in a spiritual sense, the energy surrounding it is immense. And you are all in human form, which means you are going to make mistakes in order to learn."

Reno nodded. "Well put," he rumbled. "We'd value your input on this, Fox, if you can do it?"

Shrugging, Fox said, "I'm not sure, yet, what I'll be doing in the near future." He gave Aella a reassuring look. "If possible, yes, I'd like to work with you on shaping the next mission." He gestured to his body. "First, I have to shake off the charge of energy that Guerra sent to me. I'm still weak but in the next week, I should return to full service."

Aella sat thinking how odd Fox's new situation was. Would he return to his guardian duties? Would Robert's body eventually die? She didn't want to lose him again. And now, she wished she was privy to more spiritual information than before. Calen and Reno clearly had a grasp on these heady philosophies that she did not.

"Let us know," Reno said as he held out his hand to his wife. "We're going to the hotel to get a shower and sleep. We'll talk again before we leave tomorrow afternoon."

Calen smiled gently at Aella. "You were wonderful. You got the sphere, Aella. You did everything you were asked to do. We're very grateful to you. Reno and I don't want you taking this personally, okay? You did nothing wrong. We just didn't find the right partner for you."

Getting up, Aella hugged Calen. "Thank

you," she whispered, her voice filled with tears. "I felt terrible…just terrible…."

Embracing her, Calen whispered, "I know you did. But none of this is your fault. Listen to Fox, okay?" Holding her at arm's length, Calen smiled bravely down at Aella. "We're leaving you an airline ticket. When you're ready to come down and go through the mission debrief, just hop on the plane."

The warmth and sincerity of Calen's words helped to heal some of the guilt Aella carried. Releasing the tall woman whose smile radiated through her like sunlight, she whispered, "I'll be there shortly."

Chapter 14

Aella stopped just inside the door of Fox's room. The hospital was releasing him this morning. She found him fully clothed talking to a woman in a sky-blue robe. They looked over at her as she entered.

"Aella, I want you to meet Grandmother Alaria. She's come from the Village of the Clouds."

Smiling, Aella shut the door. Instantly she felt the magical rapture permeating the room. The energy was due to this elder. She wore her silver hair plaited into two braids, and there was ageless wisdom in her peaceful face. "Hello, Grandmother Alaria."

As her hand slid into the elder's, Aella felt a frisson of incredible warmth flow up from her fingers and back to the inside of her heart.

"Child, we have been watching you from afar. It is a true pleasure to connect with you finally."

Releasing her hand, Aella smiled. "I've heard about you through Reno and Calen. Fox mentioned you too."

Alaria folded her hands within the sleeves of her simple blue robe. "Your goddess, Athena, visited me the other day."

Aella's brows raised. "She did?" Curiosity burned in her and she noticed the elder's mouth twitch with a slight smile.

"The Village of the Clouds is the only place in all worlds where those who walk the *Taqe* path to the Light are allowed entrance. We work with all the gods and goddesses of every Earth tradition who have chosen this path."

She gave a slight shrug of her proud shoulders. "Of course, there are others at that level who have chosen the *Tupay* path. Athena, your goddess, is one of us."

Relieved, Aella said, "That's good news. Why did she visit you, Grandmother?"

Alaria looked at Fox and then at her. "She has requested that you begin training at the Village of the Clouds. It is within her purview to request this for one of her priestesses. She feels you are ready for advanced metaphysical training. You will also gain deeper understanding of the karmic laws."

"Wonderful! So what does this mean? Do I have to travel?" Aella was a bit confused because she'd heard Calen discuss the village and the fact that it was not located on the Earth but in the fourth dimension.

Reaching out, Alaria briefly touched her shoulder. "In the blink of an eye, child, you'll be with us." Her voice became more firm as she glanced over at Fox. "He must come to the Village to address his soul choices. And if you want to come along, you are welcome. There is a board of inquiry into Fox's decisions and they also involve you."

Aella gave Fox a quizzical look. "Is he in trouble?"

Fox said, "Not trouble. We're allowed, as spirits, to make choices. I made some, and now a board of my elders must convene, Aella."

Aella sensed he wasn't telling the whole truth and turned to Alaria. She loved this woman without knowing why. She was the most loving, nurturing person she'd ever met. "Am I like a court witness or something?"

"In a sense," Alaria said. "We would like to hear your side of things as we assess Fox and the decisions he made."

Worriedly, Aella asked, "Will Fox be harmed in some way?"

"No, child, he will not. When a spirit either in or out of body makes choices that go counter to the laws of karma, we must try to understand why."

"Okay." Aella was still not convinced Fox wasn't in dire trouble.

"If you come, and your goddess has given permission that you may sit as a witness to Fox and his choices, we would love to have you with us."

Aella's heart tumbled with angst and uncertainty. Every time Aella looked into Fox's eyes, she felt him, not Robert. Still, it was impossible for her to get past Robert and his body. "I'm ready, Grandmother."

"Good." Alaria lifted her hands. She placed her index fingers on the centers of Fox's and Aella's foreheads. "Close your eyes. I will take you with me...."

Aella was amazed by the Village of the Clouds. When she closed her eyes, she felt a swift sense of movement, so fast that it took her breath away. When Aella was told to open her eyes, she saw a wooden bridge over a burbling stream. Jungle walls surrounded them. A narrow, well-trodden path led up to the bridge. All around, fog persisted so that all she could see was the bridge curving over to the other side of the small stream. Sounds were muted, as if she were in a vacuum.

Alaria led them across the bridge. As she walked, Aella felt a decided shift in energy. On the other side of the grassy bank, the fog began to dissipate to reveal about one hundred thatched-roofed huts of varying sizes. The further they walked down the path, the happier and lighter she felt. The people in the village were of all races. Some looked quite strange and Aella wondered if they were visiting star people from another galaxy. There were adults, children and dogs. In the distance, huge fields were tended by villagers. Beyond that, she saw a mountain chain that Fox told her was the mighty Andes.

Once in the village, Aella was met by Moyra, one of the women who lived there. She was taken to a small hut. Inside were two rooms. One had a small table and two chairs and the other a straw pallet on a hard-packed-dirt floor. After being given coconut milk, water and some fresh guavas and strawberries, Aella was asked to remain close to the hut.

Moyra, a beautiful Costa Rican woman with golden skin and long black hair, said, "I'll come back and get you in about an hour. They are convening the board of inquiry and you will be asked to attend."

Aella nodded. She was thirsty. Alone, she inspected the simple hut. Small windows allowed light and air into the rooms. Pink cotton curtains framed each one. A black-and-white cat came to the door and meowed. Aella petted it and the animal made itself at home on her pallet in the bedroom. Sitting at the table, Aella shook her head.

How had she gotten here? Obviously, magic of some sort. Aella pinched her arm. Yes, she was here in the flesh and not in spirit. Her own psychic abilities seemed enhanced to a powerful degree. When people walked by, two adults speaking a language she did not know, Aella understood them. Telepathy seemed to be utilized as much as verbal communication. If she chose to listen in on a conversation, she could. And if she wanted to shut out the mind chatter, it would cease. Amazed, Aella focused on Fox. Her gut told her he was in serious trouble. Maybe she would find out more at the board of inquiry.

Fox sat at the end of a long, mahogany table that had been hand-hewn. Its reddish surface gleamed from hours of patient polishing. On either side were four of his peers, older members of the Village of the Clouds. Alaria and Adaire sat at the other end. Fox watched as Aella was ushered in. Moyra, whom he'd met years ago, smiled hello as she led Aella to an empty chair to the right of Grandmother Alaria.

"Let us begin," Alaria told those who were gathered. "The rules are that a question will be asked and Fox will be allowed to answer without interruption. All those convened here in the name of the Great Mother Goddess understand that only the highest and best-vested interests of Fox are to be considered." Alaria glanced over at Aella. "I will call upon you at some point. Until then, simply listen and learn."

Aella nodded solemnly. She wished she didn't feel so anxious. Fox seemed relaxed and attentive, not the least bit scared or tense.

Grandfather Adaire stood. The man resembled a Druid in his cream-colored woven cotton robe, his white hair long and combed and two small braids on either side of his beard. In his hand, he held a parchment scroll.

"Atok Sopa, you are charged with deserting your post as guardian to a sacred site. You chose to send dreams to Aella that opened the portals of your lifetime with her. Lastly, you possessed a human body that was not your own. We would like to hear your reasons for such choices. Breaking the karmic law is a serious breach and we need to understand why you did so. Please speak."

Fox sat up, his hands clasped on the shining surface of the beautiful table. His voice was low as he spoke. "I fully admit that I sent Aella dreams. She was my wife, Chaska, in a Peruvian lifetime. I knew I was treading the boundaries of that law not ever to divulge a past life with another soul. I did it because my love for her never died."

"Do you regret your actions and choices?" Adaire demanded.

"I do now." Fox gave Aella a sympathetic look. "I've come to understand that my choice has done nothing but muddy Aella's view of me and her present life. I can feel her confusion. She sees the Robert Cramer she knew and is not able to see me, Atok Sopa, the spirit who inhabits that body."

"And you understand why the law regarding secrecy over past lives with another spirit are in place?" Alaria asked.

"I do now, Grandmother."

"Do you regret your choice, then?"

Fox struggled. "Grandmother, I see what I've done to Aella. I wanted her to love me as I continue to love her, but how I did it was wrong. All I've done is confuse her and that was not my intent."

"Would you do it again?" Adaire asked, setting the scroll aside.

Aella saw Fox wrestling with the question.

"I—I'm having problems with my love for her. I cannot force it to die in me, Grandparents. I have tried, but it hasn't happened."

"You were driven out of past-life obsession to reestablish connection with Aella," Alaria said quietly.

"Yes, that is so," Fox admitted. He opened his hands. "Love cannot be destroyed, and we know that. I have no explanation as to why this love for her has transcended lifetimes."

Nodding, Adaire frowned. "And because of this obsession you entered the body of Robert Cramer."

"I did. And for that, I will not ask understanding or forgiveness," Fox said. "I knew Guerra would kill Aella. I could not stand by and allow that to happen."

"Yet, that is what was asked of you," Alaria said, pinning him with a stare.

"There was no help. I had to do it."

"Are you so sure of that, Fox?" Alaria asked.

Blankly, Fox stared down at the elders. "Are you saying that if I'd passed the test of standing aside, that you would have come to help? To protect Aella?"

"My son, your test was to have faith that all would be as it should be," Alaria said. "You know at your level that absolute faith is required. We were waiting to move in to help her. It was not Aella's time to depart her body, but you didn't know this. Because you stepped in, because you broke your faith with the Great Mother Goddess's plan, the emerald sphere was taken by the *Tupay*. If you had maintained your faith and not allowed your obsessive love to get in the way of things, we would have stopped Guerra from taking the sphere as well as saving Aella's life."

Somberly, Fox considered those revelations. "I...see." He struggled to speak. "I have failed on all levels. I see that now as never before."

Adaire sighed. "My son, it is clear to us that as the test was presented to you, you are not ready to assume guardianship. Instead, there is something within your soul that still needs polishing."

Alaria looked to Aella. "Can you tell us in

your own words from your heart, how you feel about Robert and Fox?"

Choosing her words, Aella told them everything from the moment she'd taken the mission. At the end of her presentation, she added, "I'm terribly confused. I really liked Robert. He was a fine man. We got along well. And since Fox entered him, I just cannot deal with it emotionally. I see Robert, even though my heart cries out for Fox. I'm sorry, I just can't reconcile the two."

"Fox, do you see the error of your choice? That you cannot rekindle a love from a past life and make it the same in another lifetime?" Alaria asked.

Feeling the seriousness of his choice, Fox nodded. "I do, Grandmother." He looked at Aella. "I allowed my love for you to become distorted. I'm sorry that I pulled you into my wound, Aella. You deserve far better."

Tears came to Aella's eyes. She sniffed and looked at the elders. They had patient and understanding expressions on their faces. What would they do to Fox? What was his sentence?

"I don't understand the laws at my level," she told him in a quavering tone. "I feel your love. I want to respond to it. I really do. But when I feel it and then see Robert, I can't...I just don't have what it takes to make that change, Fox." She loved Fox. He knew that. And so did everyone else at this meeting.

Alaria reached out and patted Aella's hands gripped on the table. "My child, there is nothing wrong with love. Like all souls, Fox must realize this but on a wider and deeper level. He failed. Everyone at this table has failed at this very point in our development. We didn't learn it the first time we were challenged. One day Aella, you will be tested in such a way when you rise to that level."

"What is to be done with me?" Fox asked. He couldn't bear the suffering he felt around Aella. "I understand my choices and how I have not only hurt Aella but undermined the *Taqe* who try to find the Emerald Key necklace. Clearly, I have become a block in this entire process and I'm sorry from the depths of my soul. I throw myself on your wisdom to decide what you will with me." By saying that, Fox knew that he had confronted his obsessive love of Chaska. The moment he spoke those words, he felt a huge release within himself.

"You have already done it to yourself," Alaria said with a tender look in his direction. "You have finally released that life, that love, Fox."

Aella felt the energy release, too. It was as if someone had removed a cage from around her heart. The sensation was instant, but clear. Touching her breast in reaction, she stared down the table at Fox. His face had fallen and she could see the misery clearly written in his eyes.

Adaire looked around the table of two men and women who sat listening. "I ask your wisdom," he told them.

Fox sat and heard from the four elders. Finally, Adaire spoke.

"Robert Cramer's body must be given to Mother Earth," he said. "Karmically, he had chosen this path to die in this way. You can no longer inhabit his form."

Fox nodded. His mouth tightened. "I accept your wisdom."

Alaria sat up. "As you have heard, the council does not feel you are ready to resume guardianship duties, Fox."

Nodding, Fox expected the final nail to be driven into the coffin he'd created for himself. "I accept your wisdom, Grandmother."

"That means," Adaire said heavily, "that you will now descend back into the wheel of incarnations for however many lifetimes you need in order to work back up to the status you'd earned previously."

Fox knew what was coming. His heart burst with anguish because he still loved Aella. She was the twin of his soul and that would never change. Sure that the counsel would send his spirit into the Light to remain there for some indeterminate amount of time, he prepared himself never to see her again. At least, not for a long, long time, maybe centuries or thousands of years. That is what hurt him worst: Losing his twin flame. Some huge grinding machine chewed up his heart, destroying the last of his need for his cosmic partner. The one life they'd shared as Incas was it. There would be no more for some time to come, he was sure, because of his inability to separate love and faith in equal measure.

"I see you understand at the deepest level, what happened to you," Alaria said to him, her voice soft and gentle. "Suffering is all we know as a way to grow, Fox. I think I speak for everyone here at this table, when I say that you have come full circle. Your understanding of your choices, of harboring obsessive love for an individual beyond a given lifetime, has finally become clear to you."

"Yes, it has, Grandmother. Fully," Fox whispered. He looked at Aella through new eyes. Shaking his head, he gazed over at the elders. "If I had understood as I do now, I'd never have made the decisions I did out there at the Great Serpent Mound." His mouth pursed. "It will never happen again. That is my promise to my soul that I make to you, to our Great Mother Goddess."

With a slight smile, Alaria glanced over at Adaire. "Do you agree that he has embraced the honesty of his actions?"

"Indeed," Adaire rumbled. "He has."

Fox looked at Aella and saw her in a new light. Not as Chaska, but as who and what she was in this lifetime. The love he held for her was different and true and strong. He desired her—but for who she was now. In that instant, Fox realized that his honesty had set him free from the distortion and tangle of the past.

"Are you ready for the decision of the council?" Alaria asked him.

Girding himself, because Fox knew what was coming, he bowed his head and said humbly, "I am prepared for your wisdom, Grandparents."

Chapter 15

"Come with me," Alaria told Fox and Aella. She stood and thanked the other elders for attending the meeting.

Fox rose, unsure of what could happen next. He'd expected censure. A sentence of some sort other than just being demoted back to the cycle of incarnations. That punishment didn't bother him at all. He hadn't been happy as a spirit guardian. While he tried to read Alaria's closed expression, she shielded her thoughts or feelings. A sense of impending doom filled him.

They walked down a path near the wall of jungle below the village. "Is it necessary that Aella be with us, Grandmother?" Fox asked. No doubt he'd be forced to leave Robert's body and to witness this event would be more trauma for Aella.

"It is necessary, my son," Alaria said over her shoulder.

Frowning, Fox brought up the rear with Aella in front of him. She had no clue as to what was going to take place. Heart twisting in his chest, he felt helpless to protect her—once again. Sorrowfully, Fox realized that he had to surrender to a higher power and have faith. After all, the elders had pinpointed his failure in this area. So now, right now, he was being tested again.

They broke out of the jungle and in front of them was the grassy hillside. At the bottom, Fox saw a familiar sight: the Pool of Life. His confusion mounted, but he followed wordlessly.

"Ohhh," Aella said, "this is a beautiful place, Grandmother!"

"Isn't it?" She halted at the bottom of the gentle slope. Gesturing around the area, she told Aella, "We call this the Pool of Life. It's a very special body of water. Have you ever heard of it from Athena?"

"No." Aella looked into the oval, the clear depths. At the bottom was white sand, the waters were a turquoise color. "It's beautiful. It looks so inviting." She flashed a grin of appreciation.

"Would you like to go in there?" Alaria asked with a returning smile.

"Of course!"

"Then do so."

Fox scowled. "Are you going to tell her what this place is all about?" he demanded.

Alaria put her finger to her lips.

Mouth tightening, Fox realized he had no say in this. *Faith,* he told himself. *Just have faith.* This was so hard since he worried for Aella. And yet, they were in the Village of the Clouds. They were safe here. The energy here was light and healing. Fox was aware of just how distorted he'd become over the centuries. He sat down on the bank as Alaria led Aella by the elbow down to the water's edge.

"Now, my child, I want you to sit down here, take off your sandals and put your lower legs in the water. Just tell me what you feel after doing that?"

Excited, Aella sat down and quickly unbuckled her sandals and set them to one side. Eagerly, she dipped her toes into the smooth surface of the water.

Alaria stood smiling as Aella's features changed instantly. "What are you feeling?"

"Tingles!" Aella gasped. "And it's warm. Oh, this is like a very warm swimming pool! It feels like a gushing spa creating bubbles but when I look down at my legs, I see no water movement. Why?"

"It's a magical place," Alaria murmured. "Just allow the water to heal you, my child. You've been through some very hard times of late."

Aella closed her eyes. Thousands upon thousands of bubbles wrapped around her submerged legs. Energy shifted through her, and it felt as if a tidal wave moved within her body and aura. The pleasure of the energetic water made her sigh and her shoulders relaxed.

"This is wonderful, Grandmother. A few moments ago I felt heavy and fearful. Now, those feelings are gone." She looked up at the elder and grinned.

Chuckling, Alaria smiled. "This is the place where all *Taqe* are allowed to come. Some visit in their dreams to heal by bathing themselves in this living water. Others travel here astrally. And some lucky few, like yourself, are here in totality to experience the magic of these waters from the Great Mother Goddess."

"This place is incredible," Aella whispered, feeling the waves of new joy and lightness rolling through her.

"When you feel ready, pull your legs out of the water."

Aella pulled her feet out. "I'm going to drip dry," she told Alaria. Turning, she caught sight of Fox who had hung back. His face was filled with an expression of suffering. How badly she wanted to fly into his arms, embrace and kiss him. He'd made many mistakes. But who among them hadn't? Aella understood clearly that humans had to make mistakes in order to learn. The key was in trying not to repeat the mistake. She wondered privately if the test before Fox at the Great Serpent Mound was a new one. If so, his making the mistake, even at a spirit level, should not be judged harshly. Maybe Alaria had brought him here for his punishment. What kind would it be? Nothing about the Pool of Life indicated it was a sentence or a slap on the hand. She was dying to ask Alaria, but she had to remain silent out of respect for the elder.

Fox gazed at Aella as she slipped her sandals back on and stood. How beautiful she was—in this lifetime. Yes, she shared Chaska's lovely golden, slightly tilted, jaguar-like eyes and hair that shone with blue highlights beneath the sun's light, but the rest was changed. Her slender olive-colored legs shone with the last droplets of the water from her dip in the pool. He'd heard about the pool, had stood here during his training a long time ago, but Fox had never been given permission to move into its healing waters.

His gaze shifted as Alaria approached him. Her hands, as usual, were tucked into the wide sleeves of her robe. Trying to gird himself, Fox knew it was time for him to shed Robert Cramer's body. In a minute or less, he would once again be in spirit and in the fourth dimension. What happened there, he wasn't sure. Fox understood that his time with Aella was at an end. Secretly, his heart cried out in grief for the loss. No one but himself had created this situation and he had to embrace that responsibility.

"My son," Alaria began, her voice gentle, her eyes a warm blue, "you are about to embark upon a new journey."

Fox bowed his head. "Yes, Grandmother." His voice sounded weary and defeated even to him. Just standing within Alaria's considerable aura, he felt her love radiating through him, lifting him and soothing his grief. Grief that he had caused. There was no one to blame but himself.

"You understand what the Pool of Life is about? Those who come to bathe in the healing waters will be cured?"

Nodding, Fox looked past her to appreciate the beauty of the oval pool. "I was taught that those with disease could swim in the pool and be cured. That someone with emotional or mental wounding would leave the waters whole once more."

"Precisely," Alaria said, pleased. "It has other properties as well. We never speak of these to most because they are not ready for such knowledge. This morning, you are going to understand another facet of this pool's magical abilities, Fox."

He knew what was coming. Swimming in the pool would strip his spirit once and for all from the body he possessed. "I understand," he told her, his voice heavy with remorse.

Pulling a hand from her sleeve, Alaria placed

it on Fox's left arm. "My son, you do not understand. I want you to dive into the depths of the pool. Many things will happen. Things that only a higher-level soul can experience."

Fox opened his mouth to speak.

Placing her finger to her lips, Alaria smiled. "Do you have any last requests? Anything you want to say before the change takes place?"

After glancing over at Aella, he turned his full attention back to the elder. "Grandmother, my mistake was loving beyond the capacity of a given lifetime."

"Yes, my son, that is so."

"I made a mistake. That is how we learn and I know that. I cannot be sorry that I have loved the other part of my soul. I can ask forgiveness for allowing the love to turn into something that was not healthy or positive."

Giving him a tender look, Alaria whispered, "I am proud of your awareness, your growth, Fox."

"What I cannot come to grips with is that love is known to be the most powerful force in the universe. Nothing can withstand love when it is shone upon a soul."

"Just so," Alaria agreed.

"I was not wrong to love," Fox said. "I made the mistake of carrying that love beyond that lifetime."

"Exactly."

Lifting his head, he said, "I'm ready, Grandmother. I thank all of you for your wisdom and care. I fully accept my fate."

She flashed him a warm look filled with pride. "I'm going to leave now, Fox. When I am gone, I want you to dive into the Pool of Life. Only the Great Mother Goddess can determine your Fate, for we cannot. That is not our job, thankfully. It is Hers."

"I'll do as you ask," Fox murmured. He was surprised as Alaria came over to put her thin arms around his shoulders and give him a long, fierce hug.

"Never forget we love you, Fox. Where you have made mistakes, we have all made the same or similar ones. Have faith, my son.

Allow the honesty of what is to be and embrace it with a fierceness that only you can feel." She released him.

Aella smiled and hugged Alaria. She didn't understand what would happen next. Only that Fox seemed beaten and humbled. "Thank you, Grandmother, for the gift of the pool."

Alaria smoothed back a few errant strands of black hair from Aella's brow. "You're welcome, child. You are now healed. All the trauma from this experience has been absorbed by the pool's magic. Do you feel light, happy and clean?"

"Very much so," Aella whispered. She caught the elder's long, thin hand and squeezed it gently. "Thank you for everything."

Nodding, Alaria walked down the trail and was soon swallowed up by the jungle.

Fox felt as if his heart would tear out of his chest as he walked over to Aella. He loved her. It was that simple, that sweet and that unfulfilled. Gently grasping her upper arms, he said, "It's time to say good-bye. I want to wish you a life filled with happiness, Aella. Surely, you deserve it."

She frowned. "Fox, what's going on?"

"I must leave, my beloved. It is my fate." His mouth twisted as he looked over at the pool.

"No..." Aella whispered, gripping his shoulders. "Even now, I love you, Fox. I don't care what mistakes you've made. Can't we start all over?"

Fox shook his head as tears jammed into his eyes. A distraught look came to Aella's features. He forced the tears back, his voice quavering. "Beloved, you and I will always be a part of one another. No matter where we go, what incarnations we have, there will always be this quiet connection between us. Someday, we will come together. And I will look forward to that day. We were lucky to have shared one life together in Peru. Normally, twin flames do not get that opportunity."

"I love you, Fox," Aella whispered fiercely. Her hands tightened around his shoulders. "Never forget that."

Fox smiled sadly. "I want to kiss you just once, Aella, before I leave."

"Yes." She reached up on tiptoes to meet his descending mouth. His arms closed around her and never had Aella felt so loved as in this precious, fleeting moment. No longer was she kissing Robert Cramer. She was kissing the spirit within that body. As Fox's mouth moved and parted her lips, she drowned within the splendor of his tender, searching kiss. He smelled of sweat. She could feel the pounding of his heart against her breasts. His breath was ragged and warm as it flowed across her face. Most of all, Aella cherished the searching of his mouth against hers.

All too soon, the connection was broken. Aella wanted to cry as Fox released her and stepped away. His eyes were raw with grief.

Fox did not want to prolong the agony for either of them. With quick movements, he divested himself of the clothes he'd worn. Fox did not mind if Aella looked upon his nakedness. He felt strong beneath her lowered gaze.

As she stood at the edge of the grassy bank, he knew his life was about to change forever.

Without hesitation, his mouth tingling in the wake of their shared kiss, heavy with love, he dove into the pool.

Aella watched Fox knife into the clear turquoise depths. She had no idea how deep it was, but his body went beneath the water. Fox flowed to the other bank where the water became shallow, and stood in waist deep water looking toward her, confusion etched on his face.

Robert Cramer's body began to disappear. Gasping, her hands flew to her mouth. Her eyes widened as she watched. Aella saw Robert's features become like melted wax disappearing off the bones of the skull. The flesh rebuilt on the bones moments after the archeologist's face dissolved, and Aella saw another man's face emerge.

Her heart wouldn't stop its crazy beat. The face morphing into place was copper-colored, the eyes a fierce black color, large and slightly tilted. The hair grew thick and long around his broad, strong shoulders. It was his mouth that beckoned to Aella. In some deep part of herself, she remembered kissing that masculine mouth. The rest of his body reshaped itself along with his face. Fox's broad sleekly muscled chest gleamed. He grew a few inches in height, with biceps bulging, his abdomen flat and hard. His waist narrowed.

Aella had no idea how long she stood there staring dumbfounded at Fox. He seemed puzzled himself as he looked down at his new form. He ran his left hand in amazement along his lower right arm. Pinching his flesh, he shook his head. And then, he touched his long, black shining hair.

Hand against her heart, Aella crept to the edge of the pool. Fox looked so different and yet achingly familiar to her soul's memory. "Fox? What's happened?"

"By the Great Mother Goddess," he rasped in utter disbelief, giving her a stunned look.

"I'm Atok Sopa once more! This is the jaguar warrior's body I had when I lived in Peru with you. I don't believe it...." he whispered, touching his body as if making sure this was real.

Aella heard the stunned growl in his tone. "Your voice has changed, too. It's deeper. Different."

Fox's mind whirled. He lunged across the pool, swimming strongly to the other side. His hair was wet and clung to his shoulders. Without hesitation, he climbed out of the water and walked over to Aella.

"What's happened? I don't understand this."

Fox looked around. He felt the incredible energy of the pool still coursing through him like a sudden storm. A fierce pulse of life pounded through him, and he felt his powerfully beating heart. The sun warmed his wet body. The breeze made him feel the delicious touch of air upon water as it clung to his hard flesh.

Aella held his dark, black gaze. Moonlight sparkled in the depths of his large, intelligent eyes. A sense of raw nature exuded from him.

For a moment, Aella could swear she saw the head of a jaguar appearing over his face. A face with a number of scars gained from battle. And then, the jaguar was gone. Only the eyes…the eyes of a man who was really more animal, remained. "Did…did the pool give you back your life as a jaguar warrior?" she wondered in shock.

Inhaling deeply, Fox felt shaky in the aftermath of the morph. "Alaria said the Great Mother Goddess would determine my fate." He held out his arms and looked at his strong, work-worn hands. "She's given me back my warrior's body." Amazement laced his low voice. "I thought Robert Cramer's body would die and float in the pool after the silver cord was cut and I was sent back into the Light."

"That didn't happen," Aella whispered. "I saw you change, Fox. I saw Robert's form disappear. I saw the white bones of the skeleton as he dissolved into the water. And then, in its place, a new form grew upon the bones. It only took about two minutes. This is incredible."

Fox didn't know whether to laugh or cry. "I didn't know the Pool of Life could do something like this."

"Alaria said that there were other attributes to the pool and most were not aware of them." Aella looked at the pool in shock. "I guess it can do what it did for you. That's just shocking."

Fox stared at the clear, quiet depths of the pool. He touched his naked body with his hands, felt the hard flesh, the ridges of scars he'd gotten over the years in many, many battles. He was twenty-five once more, at the peak of his masculine powers shortly before he'd died in a battle.

Aella held his gaze and smiled. "Fox? I think that your mistake was only that. You were expecting a far worse punishment than you received."

Reaching out, Fox touched her curly black hair. The strands were soft and silky between his fingers. His caress brought love shining to her clear, golden eyes. "I think you're right."

"There was no punishment, Fox. You were given a gift. A gift of life…with me."

"Yes," he rasped, feeling such a fierce love of Aella, it made him breathless.

"Yes," he whispered rawly as he cupped her face and looked deeply into her eyes. "We've been rewarded. Our love for one another has transcended time. All I want is to be with you, Aella. To be at your side, share our lives together."

Fox was going to kiss her. It felt like the most right thing in her world. As she leaned upward to meet his descending mouth, her world tilted and changed forever….

Chapter 16

Aella wasn't sure of anything anymore. All she knew was that as Fox lightly brushed her lips, he was everything she wanted. The Pool of Life had stripped her of confusion. She swept her arms around his massive shoulders and drew him hard against her curves. She inhaled his male scent combined with the fresh fragrance of the pool. Strands of his hair clung to her skin, tickling her cheek as he swept her uncompromisingly into his arms.

Without a word, Fox guided her down on

the grass beside him. How right it was, Aella thought. Her mind was nearly incoherent as his mouth continued to caress her lips, open them and then deepen his kiss. His hands moved with sureness as he stripped her of her clothes. The fabric melted away from her body and in moments, her naked breasts ached for his touch. Somewhere in her soul's memory, Aella knew this Incan jaguar warrior. That knowing melded and was fully absorbed into who she was in this incarnation. This time, there was no puzzlement within her. Fox was her other half. She, the feminine part of a greater soul, he, her masculine counterpart.

As his tongue moved tantalizingly across her lower lip, his hand caressing the curve of her breast, fire arced down through Aella. Gasping as his thumb and index finger captured the nipple of her taut breast, she trembled violently. Never in her life had Aella wanted a man as much as she wanted Fox. His body covered hers and she felt the lean, hard planes grazing and claiming her. When he lifted his mouth from hers and settled his lips upon the peak of her nipple, she nearly fainted with pleasure. Making love to Fox was beyond anything she had ever experienced.

Whether it was the magic of the place that intensified all her feelings and sensations, Aella wasn't sure and didn't care. As Fox divided his attention between her breasts, her hips arched demandingly. Her flesh ground against his, lubricated by perspiration created by their hunger. Fingers digging frantically into his bunched shoulder muscles, Aella wanted to stamp her body, her mind, her pounding heart with this man who played her like a beautiful, cherished instrument.

Aella wasn't without ability either. Her hands moved down his tight ribcage. Her fingers lingered tantalizingly at his waist and then slid downward across his tense narrow hips. She sought and found the thick, dark hair between his massive thighs. As she wrapped her fingers around him, he growled—the growl of a jaguar, not a human. The sound reverberated through her like thunder spreading out across the jungle during a violent storm.

Feeling the pressure of him pushing insistently as he widened her thighs, Aella guided him into her. Pulling her hand away, she lifted her legs and encased his hips. Fox's hands settled on either side of her head as he raised his upper body away from hers. Opening her eyes, Aella drowned in his narrowed, jaguar eyes that screamed of his need for her.

Her lips tingled from his strong mouth. She smiled up at him, her fingers digging into his taut flesh. "Take me, take me…" she begged, her voice hoarse with longing.

Fox needed no other invitation. He'd held himself back, waiting for her permission. This time, he wanted Aella, not Chaska. This time, he understood with a clarity he'd not had before, that this was his mate for all lifetimes. They were being given a second lifetime together to celebrate this joyous reward and he wasn't about to miss a moment. He thrust his hips, and she cried out with pleasure, her head

tipping back, eyes closed, lips parted and curving into a satisfied smile.

As he thrust into her warm, liquid depths,
Fox felt a shattering bolt of lightning emanate
from them. The glow spread outward like a
vibrant arc and there was such rapture that
he gasped from the enormity of their ecstatic
union. No longer could he think above the fray
of their flesh meeting and melding hotly. This
very act, the act of coupling in the name of
love for one another, transcended all time and
space. For, in his heart, there was nothing else.
This was why incarnations occurred—to seek
and find this peak experience that only flesh
could create. As he swept her along with each
mighty thrust of his hips, plunging deeper into
the mystery of her depths, his heart burst open
with renewed love for her alone.

Aella's body trembled in the wake of his
sweet assault upon her, and he sensed her coming climax. Framing her face, he found and
captured her parted, wet lips. As a twin flame,
two parts of the same soul, Fox felt every

refined vibration and need within Aella. Her body convulsed with the gift of an orgasm, the warmth showering him like thick, hot honey. He took her mouth and, thrusting his tongue deep between her lips, he absorbed her on every level. He absorbed and savored the cry she uttered. And when Fox climaxed, his seed flowing deep within her, blazing white and gold lights met and combined.

For a moment that would forever be remembered by them, the burning, fierce lights they gave to one another became one. Aella clung to his mouth, feeling the pulsing vibrations sweeping through her singing flesh. This coupling was much more than just sex. It was a celebration of their spirits combining as one, finally, as never before. Whatever they had shared in their life in Peru, this was a hundred times more beautiful, sacred and brought tears to her tightly shut eyes.

Fox continued to pleasure her with his fingers and his mouth. Her body trembled violently with a series of orgasms. The intense waves made Aella limp with joy. He held her strongly and close. When at last she was utterly spent, he remained within her and brought her to his side. Her head resting upon his shoulder, brow pressed against his jaw, Aella smiled softly. Within seconds, her body vibrating like a living rainbow of light, she fell into an exhausted sleep. Safe. Loved. Forever.

Fox awoke later with Aella still in his arms. The sun had shifted position, high above them now. As he eased out of her, she awakened. Looking into her slumberous golden eyes framed by those thick, black lashes, he leaned over and caressed her lips. "I thought I knew what it was to love you, but I was wrong." He eased up on his elbow and lifted his other hand to push several damp strands of her hair off her smooth brow. "Our coming together, Aella, is on a much higher, more beautiful level."

Nodding, she had no words, but was just content to be against his masculine strength. As his fingers grazed her cheek, she whispered, "I love you, Fox. Looking back on this journey we've taken together, there wasn't a time when I didn't want you, need you."

He caught her hand and pressed a soft kiss to the back. Her black hair was curled more because of the jungle humidity, which made her that much more ravishing to him. Fox glanced at the pool. "Let's seal our fate and bathe together in the pool."

His mouth curved and his eyes danced with desire for her all over again. Aella had never made love in the water before but her body glowed brightly and wanted more of him. Rising to her feet, she took his hand. "I'm ready," she promised him, stepping to the bank.

As they sank into the arms of the water, Aella felt the millions of unseen, tantalizing bubbles surround her body. They moved into the deeper part where they swam side by side. Feeling like a child, she splashed and played. For a moment, Aella felt more dolphin than human as she dived and swam beneath the turquoise waters. The white sand below sparkled with the sunlight from above. Holding her breath, she swam a circle around Fox as he trod water. He was indeed a beautiful masculine specimen. Here and there as she rounded him with each languid stroke of her exploring hands, she saw scars he'd gained from the battles he'd fought. Her heart burst open with a fierce love as she surfaced in front of him.

Fox watched as the water slicked back her hair into short locks about her head. Her golden eyes shone with the rays of the sun within them. The love in them humbled him. As he reached out to draw her into his arms and take her to a shallower part of the pool, Fox understood the purity of what they shared. Before, when he could not release his obsessive love for Chaska, it had been a much lower expression of love. He smiled and pulled her into his arms, his toes touching the bottom. He realized that he'd grown and matured in spirit, and that this new plane of expression could be enjoyed by both of them. Their love had evolved and become something wholesome and untainted. And much, much more.

"I think that we must live this life together," Fox growled as he brought her to a place on the gently sloping sand of the pool.

Aella caressed his broad cheek. Her olive skin was a contrast to his reddish-copper flesh, but somehow, they seemed to blend and complement one another. "Yes." She held his sparkling black gaze that reminded her of the night sky. "I want to go back and help Calen and Reno. Somehow, we must support their efforts to get the rest of the emerald spheres."

"We can be of help on many levels to them," Fox agreed.

Aella languished in his arms as he lifted her and brought her next to him. Resting her head on his wet shoulder, she eased her arms around his neck. "I'd like to talk with the elders and see what they think."

"We won't do anything without their advice and direction," Fox promised. He liked standing in the chest-deep water, Aella enclosed in his arms, her body floating teasingly against his. "Are you ready to get out and start our new life together, woman of my heart and soul?"

Closing her eyes, Aella pressed a kiss to his smiling mouth. "I get dizzy just thinking about how many years we'll have with one another."

Laughter rumbled through Fox's massive chest. "It's the best sentence I could ever have received from the Great Mother. She has blessed us. All we need to do is live exemplary lives in service to others. That is the *Taqe* way."

"That is going to be so easy to do." Touching his strong mouth, she whispered, "I love you, Fox. With all my heart."

The words fell across Fox as the warm water from the Pool of Life sluiced around them. He became serious as he drowned in her wide, golden eyes. "We are one. We've always been one. We'll make this life count, I promise."

"Right now," Calen said at the mission briefing room at the foundation in Quito, Ecuador, "there is nothing we can do about the loss of the fourth sphere." She looked over at Fox and Aella. Reno sat at her elbow. For the last three hours, they'd gone over the entire mission. "We need to move forward. I've not been given a dream about where the fifth emerald sphere is located."

Aella winced. "Oh no…"

"We have to trust someone will be given the dream," Calen said.

"Adaire and Alaria said to have faith that the next emerald sphere will find the right person to find it," Reno said. "This time, we're sure whoever the sphere chooses will have strong psychic abilities so that they can be aware of the threat of the *Tupay*. We showed the spheres that we made a poor choice with your team, Aella. It's out of our hands now."

"I understand," Aella said quietly. "Robert was a good man."

"No question," Calen said, regret in her voice. "But he didn't have the necessary psychic tools. It wasn't his fault. He gave his life for this mission and he's a hero in our eyes."

"I'm sure his spirit is already very happy somewhere in the fourth dimension," Fox told them. "He's free of a human body and all that it means. According to many people's beliefs here on Earth, he is in heaven, so to speak."

"Yes," Aella said with a gentle smile, remembering Robert. "I know he's happy now. And that makes me feel better."

"I talked with Grandfather Adaire yesterday," Reno told them. "He gave me an update on Robert's spirit. Adaire wanted all of us to know that his spirit has chosen to serve the *Taqe* and their mission to regain the emerald spheres. Robert gave his life for those ideals. He's at peace with this lifetime. His relatives were notified of his passing, and now, he's an advocate for us."

"Good, we can use his help," Fox murmured, placing his hand upon Aella's. They sat together opposite Reno and Calen. "We would like to be part of the continuing mission. You may use us as you see fit. In the long term, we may be able to help you in some way to recover the lost fourth sphere."

Reno nodded. "We're more than happy to have you work for the foundation. Right now, we need to focus on getting the fifth sphere. Guerra, I'm sure, is very pleased with the theft of the fourth one. And this will make him even bolder in trying to steal the next one. We have an enemy that is powerful, cunning and will stop at nothing to get them."

Calen gave her husband a tender look. "No one said it would be easy recovering these spheres. We understand that this is about the difference between humans choosing Light over the heavy energy of the *Tupay*. We'll do our part the best we know how."

"And it doesn't promise victory," Reno told the group. "There was never that guarantee by the Great Mother as to who would finally retain the necklace."

Fox sighed. "Throughout Earth's history, there has always been a tug-of-war between Dark and Light. The heavy energy of the Dark, those people who are not yet awake, who do not realize the implications of being asleep, makes a willing army for Guerra. He's powerful. And right now, anyone could win the necklace."

Calen stood and said, "We know because of our failure that the emerald sphere will choose a candidate for the next mission. Let's adjourn for some lunch and then we'll meet back here after siesta."

That sounded fine to Fox. Rising, he gripped Aella's hand. "Lead the way."

As they padded in sandals along the hardwood floor toward Calen and Reno's kitchen, Fox slid his arm around Aella's shoulders. She looked up and love shone in her eyes for him alone. It made him feel incredibly powerful in a masculine way.

"Are you ready for our new life together?" he teased.

"Completely. I had a dream last night. My goddess Athena came to me and she said that I must continue to visit the Village of the Clouds and learn the next level of spirit information."

"Good," Fox praised as they walked down a spiral staircase to the bottom portion of the home. "It will only help you expand your knowledge."

"I know you're already there, but I'll catch up fast," she said.

"You've earned this right, Aella." At the bottom of the stairs, he placed his hands on her shoulders. "Despite our setbacks, our losses and mistakes, we've been blessed."

"Isn't that the way it always is here on Earth?" she posed, appreciating his male beauty, that rugged mouth of his, those alert, large eyes that were more jaguar than human.

"Always." Turning, Fox led her down another hall toward the kitchen where he could smell food cooking. "Our mission is to lift Earth's energy onto a lighter plane. And I know we can do this."

Her arms wrapped around his narrow waist. "Together," she promised him, her voice husky with emotion. "Forever..."

* * * * *

Don't miss Lindsay McKenna's next novel,
The Adversary, *available February 2011*
from Mills & Boon® Nocturne™.

Something is wrong with Kaylee Cavanaugh…

She can sense when someone near her is about to die. And when that happens, an uncontrollable force compels her to scream bloody murder. Literally.

Kaylee just wants to enjoy having caught the attention of the hottest boy in school. But when classmates start dropping dead for no reason and only Kaylee knows who'll be next, finding a boyfriend is the least of her worries!

Book one in the Soul Screamers series.

Available 1st January 2011

www.mirabooks.co.uk

FREE BOOK
AND A SURPRISE GIFT

We would like to take this opportunity to thank you for reading this Mills & Boon® book by offering you the chance to take a specially selected book from the Nocturne™ series absolutely FREE! We're also making this offer to introduce you to the benefits of the Mills & Boon® Book Club™—

- **FREE home delivery**
- **FREE gifts and competitions**
- **FREE monthly Newsletter**
- **Exclusive Mills & Boon Book Club offers**
- **Books available before they're in the shops**

Accepting this FREE book and gift places you under no obligation to buy, you may cancel at any time, even after receiving your free book. Simply complete your details below and return the entire page to the address below. You don't even need a stamp!

YES Please send me a free Nocturne book and a surprise gift. I understand that unless you hear from me, I will receive 3 superb new stories every month, two priced at £4.99 and a third larger version priced at £6.99, postage and packing free. I am under no obligation to purchase any books and may cancel my subscription at any time. The free book and gift will be mine to keep in any case.

Ms/Mrs/Miss/Mr _____ Initials _____

Surname _____

Address _____

_____

_____ Postcode _____

E-mail _____

Send this whole page to: Mills & Boon Book Club, Free Book Offer, FREEPOST NAT 10298, Richmond, TW9 1BR